THE
NIGHT
GUEST

THE
NIGHT
GUEST

HILDUR KNÚTSDÓTTIR

TRANSLATED BY MARY ROBINETTE KOWAL

TOR PUBLISHING GROUP
NEW YORK

NIGHTFIRE

THE NIGHT GUEST

Translation by Mary Robinette Kowal

This book has been translated with financial support from:

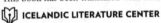 ICELANDIC LITERATURE CENTER

A Nightfire Book
Published by Tom Doherty Associates / Tor Publishing Group
120 Broadway
New York, NY 10271

www.torpublishinggroup.com

Nightfire™ is a trademark of Macmillan Publishing Group, LLC.

The Library of Congress Cataloging-in-Publication Data is available upon request.

ISBN 978-1-250-32204-3 (hardcover)
ISBN 978-1-250-32250-0 (ebook)

Our books may be purchased in bulk for promotional, educational, or business use. Please contact your local bookseller or the Macmillan Corporate and Premium Sales Department at 1-800-221-7945, extension 5442, or by email at MacmillanSpecialMarkets@macmillan.com.

First published as *Myrkrið milli stjarnanna* in 2021 in Iceland by JPV.

First U.S. Edition: 2024

Printed in the United States of America

0 9 8 7 6 5 4 3 2

THE
NIGHT
GUEST

|

"Can you describe your symptoms?"

I clear my throat. "I'm just so . . . *tired* all the time."

"Not sleeping well?"

"No, no. I fall asleep and even sleep through the night. But when I wake up, I feel exhausted. My legs, my arms . . ."

As if they were evidence, I extend both arms. My hands dangle limply, and I have the bizarre impulse to shake them in the doctor's face. But she nods. When I lower them, they drop into my lap like dead pieces of meat.

"I don't feel like I'm waking up rested but more like I've been out on a rampage all night. My muscles are worn out. Not soreness like after working out, but sort of like when you've been slogging away at something and can tell that the next day you're going to really feel it, you know?"

"And it's only in the arms and legs?"

"Not only, but mostly there. I'm tired all over. Even my jaw."

The doctor nods again.

I like her. She's probably ten years younger than I am. If I had to guess, I'd say she probably hasn't finished her residency yet. Which means she's being very thorough. She will not let acute lymphocytic leukemia or some horrific neurological disease slip past her. She's going to check out every possibility. Which is precisely what I want and what the previous doctor the health center assigned me to—some old, gray-haired prick—refused to do.

That guy had clearly had enough of women with unexplained symptoms. *Hysterical* women. I seriously wanted to lecture him about all the diseases women have had that have been misdiagnosed over the years—and how medication (not to mention everything else in this world) is designed for the male body—but I just didn't have the energy for it. Or maybe I was chicken. Or maybe that's the same thing because it's a lot easier to gather your courage when you're not dead tired.

When I left the prick's office with orders to go home and "take it easy" for two weeks (he didn't even suggest seeing a therapist, probably because he's too old to believe in psychology), I made a beeline for the health center's reception desk and asked for an appointment with a female doctor.

"Someone young," I said. The receptionist looked at me like I was off my rocker but still gave me an appointment with this new doctor.

Her name is Ásdís, and she has blond hair and two

pimples on her chin that she's done her best to cover with concealer. "Has this been going on for a long time?"

"A while, yeah. And getting worse."

"Have you had the flu recently? Any kind of cold?"

"No."

"Have you been under a lot of stress lately?"

I think about Stefán and how he had hissed at me that I was a bitch right before slamming the door in my face. How I had trembled like a twig in the wind and hadn't been able to bring myself to move for over an hour after he left.

"No." Stefán is a lousy guy, but I'd be giving him way too much credit if I blamed this on him.

"Do you eat a variety of foods?"

"Yes. I'm a vegetarian, but that's not new. And I take B12, omega-3, and iron."

She glances at the computer screen. "I see you had blood work done six months ago. Everything looks good there. But we'll run it again." Ásdís turns back to me with her full attention. She wears an expression that is at once concerned and kind. "With what I have here, I don't see anything to indicate a serious condition. Not based on your history or my examination. So, tell me, what are you concerned about?"

A sensation begins to stir in my belly. Warm and soft. And I realize that I'm weirdly proud of her. Ásdís is going to be a truly wonderful doctor. For a moment, I feel as though I am her mother (Christ), or maybe a grandma (*Christ!*), who watched her grow up through childhood and then become an unbearable teenager who blossomed into an intelligent woman who attended medical school and now speaks to her patients with respect and genuine concern. I almost tear up.

And then, I remember the fear that had overcome me as I sat and googled my symptoms.

"Myasthenia gravis," I blurt. "Or . . ." I hesitate. Then I speak the acronym that's been haunting me over the past few days. "ALS."

Ásdís nods. I begin to sweat. Recently, I've been almost entirely convinced that I'm doomed to this future: experiencing my nervous system's gradual failure. I've wondered how it might feel when parts of my body stop working, one after the other. Maybe it starts with numbness in my fingertips. Then I lose control of my hands, followed by my arms. Then my feet. Then I'll lose all sensation below the waist. Stop being able to turn my head, speak, smile, blink my eyes. Maybe I'll learn to hold a brush with my mouth and paint a few pictures. Then my respiratory system will stop working, and I'll die.

Ásdís cocks her head. "I don't want to sound dismissive of your experience, but I have to say that it strikes me as . . . an extremely unlikely diagnosis."

Relief washes over me like the sea.

"Really?"

"Yes."

"So, you don't think I've got some terrifying neurological disease?" I ask, just to hear her say it one more time.

"No. Of course, I can't rule it out, but I don't see anything to indicate it."

Another wave of elation.

Then I remember what I was going to show her.

"What about leukemia?" I stand up and tug my pants down, showing her the large bruise on my hip that had appeared overnight. "Don't you think it looks a little like spotting?"

Ásdís puts on gloves. She aims the tabletop lamp at me and leans over my hip. She runs her fingers over the bruise, so close that I can feel her warm breath moving the fine hairs on my skin. My god, she's doing a thorough job. It crosses my mind that I might be in love with her, which is a little ridiculous.

"Did you bump into something?" she asks.

"No, I woke up like this."

The bruise is the size of a little pancake.

Ásdís sits up and points the lamp back at the desk. I pull up my pants and take a seat.

"This appears to be a standard hematoma. But I'll add a white blood cell count to your blood work. And we'll look at your iron levels, of course."

Ásdís stands up. The examination has come to an end. She extends her hand, her grasp firm and professional. She's taller than I am, and yet I have this urge to pat her on the head or the cheek. I restrain myself.

Instead, I thank her and leave.

When I get home, Mávur is curled up on the porch in front of the door. The cat stands when he spots me, his tail rising with pleasure. I scratch him behind the ears, and he responds with a loud purr. He often tries to sneak in, but I know his tricks and am quick to shut the door behind me. By the time the latch catches, he has already lain back down, his eyelids drooping in the sunshine.

I know that the world's sorrows are both abundant and profound and that a cat allergy is perhaps insignificant in the larger scheme of things. But there is something so unfair about loving cats and being relegated to do so from a distance.

2

Three days later, I receive a text saying that I have a message from the health center waiting for me. I open the medical portal and am asked to log in with my electronic ID. Like every Icelander, I have my *kennitala*, of course, but I'd never linked my national ID number with an online account. So I don't have an electronic ID. Someone—I don't remember who—told me they were just a plot to force all Icelanders into a monopoly with a cousin of some Progressive Party big shot in perpetuity. Or was it the Independence Party?

And the banks seem to be in on it, too, because they provide the ID numbers. When you think about it, it's a little odd that banks generate our government IDs, but that's commonplace Icelandic corruption for you.

I call the health center and request the results by phone. The woman who answers at the front desk says it's not available. She says it in an offensively cheerful tone. I grumble at her, but she just gets cheerier.

During my lunch break, I go to the bank. All the

muscles in my thighs ache when I walk up the stairs. I feel like I've been on a treadmill all night. (For the record, I have never used a treadmill.)

Two women are standing in the lobby of the bank and welcome me. I notice that there is only one cashier but at least four employees who seem to be working on linking *kennitalas* with electronic ID accounts.

It's easier to get one than I expected. The man who helps me makes me sign some papers that I'm too tired to bother reading. He's the officious sort who wants to cover his ass by making it "quite clear" that page three states that the service is free now but that he cannot rule out the possibility that it will have a fee later.

"Yes, I know everything about the Progressive Party," I say, though, of course that's not true.

He gives me a weird look. Maybe it was the Independence Party, after all. But I mean, really, what's the difference?

THE FIRST THING I do when I get back to work is to log into the health center. There's a message from Ásdís María Ómarsdóttir waiting for me. I feel warm inside just seeing her name. Then I take a deep breath and open the mail from her.

All the blood tests came out well. All results normal.

I stare at the message for a long time. When the letters start to blur, I realize that I'm—damn it—crying.

I sniff, wipe my cheeks, and glance around me. Fortunately, almost everyone is still at lunch, and no one seems to have noticed anything.

I get to my feet, go to the toilet, and clean myself up.

The lump in my throat swells. Staring at my reflection above the sink, I tell myself not to cry.

It's not that I was hoping I was sick.

Except maybe I was just hoping for . . . something. Not ALS—never ALS—and not myasthenia gravis. But maybe something innocent. Iron deficiency, iodine deficiency, arthritis, some manageable metabolic disease, B12 deficiency—or perhaps a little hypoactive thyroid. Was that too much to ask?

Because there is nothing worse than having unexplained symptoms. *Feeling* like there's something terribly wrong—but nothing that can be measured in exams, and you know the doctor thinks it's all in your head.

I stare at my reflection, reminding myself, of course, that it could be much worse. The tests came out well. I should not be disappointed. I should feel relieved.

"You should be happy," I hiss at the mirror.

And to my surprise, the trace of a malicious grin twists the side of my mouth.

"I'm not hysterical," I tell my reflection.

She nods.

3

I increase my vitamin dose. Also, buy vitamin D. And calcium and something called spirulina that the girl in the pharmacy recommends. Then I google and read that spirulina can contain large amounts of heavy metals, so I throw it in the trash. My conscience twinges about throwing it in the trash (The heavy metals, where do they go? Landfills? Maybe into the groundwater?), but I don't do anything about it.

I go to the bar with my friends after work. They say I need to be more active.

"That's how you get energy! Not by lounging on the couch! I could explode after I ran ten kilometers! I felt like I could conquer the world," says Ásta. She's the CEO of a large company and has three children. She probably often feels like she can conquer the world.

"Go to yoga," says Linda. "You just have to relax. Don't you have too much to do at work? And you have tried essential oils?"

"Why don't you just go eat some meat? We're not meant to live on vegetables alone, you know," says María, and takes a sip of white wine.

Looking grave, they all nod.

"But we don't have true canines," I point out.

They stare at me over their wineglasses.

"Carnivores all have canines."

They glance at each other, not sure what to do with me, and an embarrassing silence stretches between us.

This always happens. Everyone will be having a good chat until I say something wrong and feel as though I've been exposed as the alien in the group. *Ta-da! Did you think I was one of you? Hahaha!*

I don't know if it's because they're all the same age—two years older than I am—or because I joined their group late. Maybe it's something different and more profound. I don't remember whether I've always felt this way or if the feeling has gradually worsened.

"I know it sounds like the name of a cartoon character," says Helga. "But Zumba literally saved my life after pregnancy."

I take a big sip of red wine (rich in iron).

"Try walking more," says Sigrún. "I read somewhere that walking is—by far—the healthiest exercise. You just need to walk ten thousand steps a day!"

"What happened there?" Ásta points to the bruise on my chest.

I had specifically chosen a shirt that would cover it.

But now I look down and see that as I bend forward, my neckline is gaping, and the bruise is visible. It's a tiger stripe of dark purple.

I straighten and pull my collar up.

"Nothing." Which is technically true.

They look at each other with worry wrinkles between their eyebrows. *Ta-da! Unmasked again!*

Helga places a palm over my hand. "Was that Stefán?"

"No." I laugh.

"You know you can tell us anything," she says understandingly.

Their nods are full of grave disbelief.

I take another sip of red wine.

Two minutes of "happy hour" are left when I finish my drink. At the bar, I see a man. He's wearing a pale pink shirt (confident about his masculinity) and a blue, well-fitting jacket, and he's staring at me like he's seen a ghost.

I get embarrassed and look down at the drink list. When I look up again, he has half-turned away from me and is waving a credit card over a beer that the waiter is handing to him.

Then he looks back at me.

I'm trying to decide if I should smile politely or pretend not to see him, but I haven't figured out what to do when he turns away and walks with his beer to a nearby table. Around it, well-dressed men sit, stretched out in low chairs (why do men always have to take up so much space?) and laughing.

4

The watch costs a fortune. The clerk tells me that this is the most accurate pedometer in the store. "And all over the country, actually."

"Is it really?"

"You can send the data automatically to a computer. Put it in a graph or display it any way you want. Or automatically post your stats straight to Facebook. The GPS device is also extremely accurate."

"Is this spyware?" I've read articles about the threats of modern technology to personal security. All the data these devices collect. And who knows who's sitting at the other end watching.

"Huh?"

"Is it easy to hack into a watch? I've heard that some of these watches aren't safe. And if someone hacks it, can they tell where I am?"

"It's completely secure." Then he hesitates, and casually raises his hand as if to hedge his bets and draw a warranty in the air. "Or—as safe as they get. The safest we have. The safest in the country."

"Yeah." I squint. I don't think he looks like he knows exactly what he's talking about. He's got gel in his hair, and the light blue shirt he's wearing seems to have been freshly ironed that morning. And he smells really good—I can smell him even though he's about three meters away. Shouldn't tech salesmen be . . . nerdy?

"But of course, you don't have to have it turned on," he says. "The location, the automatic transmissions, and so on. That's all just a matter of configuration. You can set it as you see fit."

I buy the watch.

When I get home, I read the instruction booklet carefully. I turn off all activity except the pedometer. Then I put the watch on my bedside table.

5

The mornings are the hardest. I wake up tired. I feel like the hand I use to turn off the alarm weighs at least fifty kilos (I'm fifty-five myself). I can't open my eyes immediately. It's always an effort. I lie like a log, all my muscles wooden. My joints are stiff and full of sand, like an old toy that someone has forgotten on the playground overnight.

It's not exactly a pain I feel, but it's not a non-pain either. The feeling is something in between. Both and. Neither nor.

Sometimes I take painkillers so I can start the day. They never work. I don't even get the placebo effect that I read about which is supposed to affect about 20 percent of people. Honestly, I think it's totally unfair that I'm not one of them. But of course—when I consider it more—I realize I lack the magic ingredient for this formula: the belief that painkillers can help me.

I drink herbal tea instead of coffee. My mom's friend told her I should try cutting caffeine. "It changed my life!" she asserted, according to my mother. I have not drunk coffee for two weeks. I haven't felt any difference, if anything I'm possibly worse. Even more tired.

I shuffle toward the shower. It's difficult to lift my legs over the edge of the bathtub. Sometimes I imagine that one day my foot will slip and I'll fall and injure myself horribly. This is probably how it feels to get old. I once read about an old woman in France who lived alone. One day she fell inside her bathroom and broke her thigh. And she lay there for *days,* screaming for help and knocking on the wall before the neighbors finally heard her.

My hand turning on the faucet is heavy, and my fingers are stiff. I close my eyes. At least the water is warm. Maybe I'm one of those people who needs to learn to appreciate the little things in life. Let them suffice.

The smell of my shampoo is good. It's just so hard to rub it into my hair. The smell of the conditioner is even better. But I don't have the energy to use it now.

I turn off the water. Then stand for what must be a whole minute and let it drip off me. I'm hardening my mind to cope with the day. I haven't fully succeeded when I have to leave.

I just barely remember the watch on my bedside table.

THERE ARE 3,728 steps to my job. Then I walk to the store for lunch and buy myself a sandwich. There are 815 steps, back and forth. On the way home to my apartment, I take a big detour down Sæbraut. When I get home, I've walked 9,568 steps. I'm so tired that I'm just going to lie down on the sofa and not get out of it except to open the door for the pizza delivery driver later tonight.

6

"New watch?" Stína asks. "Is this a Garmin?"

She's sitting at the desk next to mine. I'm always startled by what she notices and does not notice. She didn't say anything when I underwent laser surgery two years ago and stopped wearing glasses. She also never seems to notice when I go for a haircut or dye my hair. But if I get new shoes, she spots them immediately. Once, when my mother gave me a sample of a new perfume (she goes to all kinds of women's nights at the Smáralind mall and god knows where else women's nights take place; she comes back loaded with tiny jars and tiny perfume bottles and pushes them on me) Stína lifted her head and sniffed the air like a bloodhound as I walked through the door. She hadn't even looked at me when she shouted, *"J'adore Eau de Parfum!"*

Maybe she's just more interested in brands than people.

I shrug. "I only needed a pedometer. The guy in the shop recommended this."

Stína rolls her eyes at me. "You haven't started run-ning?"

"I'm walking."

"Why not use the pedometer in your phone?"

"Huh?"

"Don't you have an iPhone? Why don't you use the pedometer in it?"

"There's a pedometer in the iPhone?"

Stína rolls her eyes again. Sometimes I suspect that she thinks I am a complete idiot. Other days I'm sure of it.

"Yes. In Health."

I stare at her. She extends her hand. "Let me have your phone."

I obey.

She rolls her eyes again, thrusting the phone back toward me. "You need to unlock it first."

I pick up the phone, unlocking it, and hand it to her again. She opens an app that I don't think I've thought to open. Something with a heart icon.

"See!" She shows me a calendar. Then picks yester-day and hands the phone back.

9,472 steps are displayed on the screen.

"Oh," I say. "But they don't agree."

Stína snorts. Then she shakes her head tiredly, as if I'm beyond helping.

1

I wake up with the taste of blood in my mouth. When I stumble into the bathroom and look in the mirror, I see a rust-red spot on my chin. I wet toilet paper and use it to wipe the stain off. The paper turns red. This is blood. I'm sure of it. I examine my lips, tongue, and gums, but I don't see any sores.

My jaw aches. Like I've been chomping on something all night. The pain stretches to my cheekbones, up behind my eyes and locks into the back of my skull like a giant claw.

The watch cost ISK 44,900.

I decide to use it rather than the phone. I know it doesn't really justify the purchase, but I still feel better about it somehow.

I have walked ten thousand steps a day for the last seven days. Ásta claims that I should be full of energy, but if anything, I'm even more tired.

I book another doctor's appointment. Ask especially for Ásdís.

8

"I don't feel any better," I say.

This sounds like an accusation, although it's not meant to be. I know she's done everything in her power. I don't know exactly what I expect from her but I'm hoping she's more imaginative than I am. I've read everything I've found on the internet. But she has to have read so much more.

Fortunately, Ásdís does not seem to take my complaint to heart, and only strokes her chin thoughtfully. Something about the movement reminds me of an old man, and I'm so glad she's not an old man.

"I'm sorry to hear that." She turns to the computer, looking at something there. "All the blood tests came out well. . . . Still the same symptoms?"

"Yes."

"And nothing has changed?"

I consider telling her about the bloodstain on my chin, but I don't.

"No. I'm still trying to be active," I say, in order to say something.

"That's good. Do you think it's helping?"

"No."

"Are you under stress?"

"No."

"Have you been depressed?"

"No. Or, rather, it's not fun to be tired all the time. I can't do much. And I'm worried. But that came later. The other came first."

"I'm going to ask you to take this test." Ásdís hands me a piece of paper and a pencil. "I'm checking something in the meantime."

Then she gets to her feet and walks away. I look at the paper.

How often has the following happened to you in recent weeks?

1. I have experienced melancholy and hopelessness.

The possible answers are: *Never, sometimes, more than half the time, almost daily*.

I circle *more than half the time*.

2. I have no appetite and have difficulty eating.

I circle *never*.

3. I have a difficult time keeping track of what I'm doing.

Almost daily.

I'm long since finished with the exam when Ásdís returns.

She writes a number after each answer and then adds

them up at the bottom of the page. "I'd like you to talk to a psychologist. You're showing a few signs of depression."

"A lot?"

"Nothing terrible, not life-threatening. But more than a little. Do you think you could meet with a psychologist?"

"Do you think it will help? With the symptoms? The fatigue? The muscle pain?"

"It might. Would it be okay to try?"

"I guess so."

Ásdís recommends a psychologist. His name is Þórir Skúlason, and he has an office in Ármúli.

I google him when I get home. The office he works at is called the Psychology Institute (how original). There is a picture of him on their website. Þórir Skúlason seems to be around forty and he looks like a handball player (blond, broad shoulders, receding hairline). He's very handsome. He specializes in depression, anxiety, and working with the chronically ill.

There's an online form for booking an appointment with the Psychology Institute, which is very nice for anxiety patients, I expect.

I do not book an appointment.

9

My knee hurts when I wake up. Lifting my leg, I feel a burning sensation in my calf and thigh. I open my eyes. Something is not right. At first, I think it's the light. Maybe I've woken up too early, but I can make out sunlight on the other side of the curtains. A strip of light falls on the white wall overhead. I glance at the clock. I've awoken eight minutes before the alarm. There's something bothering me. An odor.

My pillow gives off a cold and briny scent. I feel a lock of my hair. It's damp under my fingertips. I pull it to my nose and inhale deeply. My hair smells like the sea. As though I have been down at the shore while a strong wind blew in off the water.

I must have sweated profusely overnight. Did I have a nightmare? I don't remember my dreams anymore.

When I stand up, my back is sore. It's as if there were a red-hot cord running up my spinal column. I take off my shirt and underpants, toss them in the hamper, and head to the bathroom.

I sit down to pee and as I reach out to take some

toilet paper my gaze falls on my watch. I had forgotten to take it off before I went to sleep. I freeze when I see the number on the screen.

47,325 steps.

I took the bus to work yesterday morning and then I walked home. It was only about 6,000 steps. And then the watch resets at midnight. This can't be right.

47,325 steps.

The watch must be broken.

10

I reset the watch manually and then walk to work. As soon as I sit at my desk, I start googling. This must be a known design flaw. But I only find people complaining that the battery doesn't work well in the cold and that the Bluetooth connection doesn't reach far enough. I google myself blue but I can't find anything about it miscounting a person's steps. Not a thing.

When it's nearly lunchtime, I decide to quit. I send a Facebook message to the store where I bought the watch and then check my work email. The top message is from my ex, Stefán. I feel sick to my stomach. But when I open it, it's just some mass email he's sent to everyone in the company because some people have not been saving things correctly to the shared drive. The tone of the post is very kind, and there are ten screenshots that show exactly how to do it right. He's photoshopped in all kinds of arrows and notes for guidance. It must have taken him a long time.

For the past few weeks, I have been avoiding the cafeteria and the third floor, where he works. I've only seen him twice since that Friday. The first time was at a large staff meeting. Then he sat in the corner, at the back, and I made sure never to look in his direction. The second time, I glimpsed him as he disappeared around the corner next to the stairwell in the lobby while I walked to the elevator one morning. I suspect he's avoiding me too.

I go out to Krónan and buy myself a sandwich and a bottle of mineral water. Using a plastic bottle troubles me—but the mineral water machine is in the cafeteria on the third floor.

I eat the sandwich in the little break room on our floor and flip through Instagram. When my phone beeps, I startle. It's a message from the store where I bought the watch. They don't recognize this error. But if I want, I can bring the watch in and they can send it out for repairs.

WHEN I GET home, I've walked 9,385 steps. I manually reset the watch when I take it off before I go to bed. Then I put it on the bedside table.

The next morning it's still zero.

II

I don't brag about it to anyone, but I know all the cats in the neighborhood. Or okay, not *all* of them. Most. Those who have lived here for more than a few weeks and aren't just wandering through. On our neighborhood page on Facebook, people often post a picture with something like: "Does anyone know this unmarked cat? He's been coming to our house and . . ." Blah blah blah.

Almost every time, I could comment with something like: "Yes, yes, this is Mávur, he lives in the house next door" or "That's Sushi, she's just a little upset because her owners got a dog, but she'll get used to it."

But I do not.

Because there's another woman in the neighborhood group who owns a microchip reader (why?), and I don't want to deny her the joy of running around the neighborhood, identifying the strays. She must get a lot out of it, because she's constantly present in the comments, offering her help. Besides, I'm not the type who comments a lot in large groups. I never really post anything on Facebook, just use it to spy.

I know the cats. And they know me. If I see one of them, it's usually enough to just cluck my tongue and say "kiskis" and then they come running. But lately, it seems like they've begun to distrust me. A few days ago Brandur (yes, just like from *Kitten Brandur,* the children's book that taught most of us to read) arched his back when he spotted me, and now Tigger Tiggersson (yes, his real name) just stands and stares at me suspiciously when I call. And when I approach, he lowers his head and hisses.

Tigger Tiggersson and I have known each other for eight years. He's never acted like this before.

Maybe he's scared by the bag I'm carrying. It's a grocery bag from Bónus, the environmentally friendly kind that's supposed to break down in nature and also wears out as soon as you start using it. Or maybe the perfume I've been using lately (trial from Mom) is to blame?

"Kiskis," I call and cluck. Tigger Tiggersson hisses again. Then he backs away, shoots under a fence, and disappears.

When I get home, I google the name of the perfume plus cats but can't find anything.

12

I'm going to my mom and dad's for dinner. The meals there always follow a well-rehearsed script, with occasional variations according to the seasons and the physical condition of those present.

"How is work?"

"Fine, just fine."

"Always so much to do?"

"Yes." Smile. "Anything new with you?"

"No, not a thing. Except, of course, your dad has a bad back."

"Is that so?"

"Yes. Palli, tell her how bad it is."

"Very bad."

"I'm sorry to hea—"

"I have already told him that he must be more diligent about going swimming. Have I not said that to you, Palli?"

"Yes, but—"

"And he needs to go to a physical therapist, too, have I not been telling you to go to a physical therapist too?"

"Yes, but—"

"The waiting lists are just so long."

"Is that so?"

"Yes."

"Have you started planning your summer vacation?"

"No, but—"

"We are thinking of going to Florence."

"Is that—"

"But your dad really wants to play golf. We've asked Hedda and Geir if they want to come. But I don't know if his back can handle it."

"The trip?"

"No, golf."

"Yes, I can stand it—"

"But it must be very humid there."

"Really?"

"Your sister always told me she wanted to go to Florence."

"I know."

"I think we should go, together."

"Mhm."

"Don't you want to come?"

"No, I don't think so."

"A little sun might do you good."

"Can I have more red wine?"

"Don't you want more chicken?"

"Mom, I don't eat—"

"Yes, oh, right. At least you can have more rice and a

little sauce. I think it was a vegetable bouillon cube that I put in it."

"Shall we open—?"

"Palli, go open another bottle of red wine please."

After dinner, Dad offers me a beer. A giant can of Viking beer. I drink one in front of the TV (Gísli Marteinn's latest talk show), and as soon as I swallow the last sip I realize that the beer and the three glasses of red wine mean that I'll probably be hung over tomorrow. After a dinner with my parents. Where there were just the three of us, and I ate rice with sauce and went home before ten o'clock.

There is nothing in the world more tragic than an undeserved hangover. So I text Linda (my only childless friend) and ask if she'd like to meet.

LINDA IS ONE of those people who goes to sushi restaurants and orders nothing but tiny pieces of beef. She's been at the restaurant for over an hour with two friends I only know from parties she's thrown. They went to college together and they seem nice enough.

Linda said I should meet them for dessert, but I'm still hungry after dinner, so I order an avocado sushi roll and a glass of white wine. They get balls of ice cream, coated in chocolate that melts as you pour a hot caramel sauce over it.

While we eat, they talk about people who went to

school with them. I try to keep track. It's just a little hard to gossip about people you've never met.

One story is still a bit juicy. A man they know was cheating on his wife. There was an "oops" pregnancy, and now all three of them are raising the baby together: the husband, the mistress, and the wife.

"These must be very good people," I say.

They look at me in shock.

"At least the wife."

Linda smiles. "Somehow you always manage to look on the positive side; I adore that."

I stare at her in amazement. I have *never* been told this before. I've always stood firm in the belief that I'm a very negative person. That's a big part of my identity.

"How else have you been?" she asks, as if offering an invitation to air my troubles.

"Just fine," I lie, and then grab the last piece of sushi. I do not bother to tell her friends about all my woes.

"Maybe we should go to a bar?" says the blonde with her hair in a bun, who is so terribly thin that you can count the ribs on her chest. Lately I've tried not to be judgmental, but . . . she didn't eat any of her dessert. She just stirred it a little, licked the spoon, and then placed a napkin over the melted ice cream. And some part of me is pleased. Because this woman might be more beautiful than I am, better educated, in a better job, with more money than I have, and she probably has also a great husband and beautiful children. But she's still unhappy with herself (I'm a terrible person).

"Absolutely!" say the others in chorus.

Linda looks at me. "Aren't you coming?"

"Of course," I say.

WE'RE GOING TO a bar that I had no idea existed. It's downtown on the top floor of a building on Austur-stræti. There are silver tables, tall chairs, and deep sofas that hold beautifully dressed people. These are people who have money, or at least make an effort to look like they do. My head hurts and my shoulders ache, as if thin glowing cords have started to grow out of my shoulder blades up to my neck and stretch down toward my elbows. The only solution in this situation is to drink more. Something strong and a lot of it. I'm going to feel miserable tomorrow anyway (I always feel miserable) and nothing I do from now on will matter at all. I follow the girls to the bar and order a glass of white wine and a shot of vodka.

The vodka shot burns my throat. I cough, pick up the glass of white wine, and then I see him. The man I saw at "happy hour." The one who stared at me so oddly. He does it here too. He stands at one of the tall silver tables and stares. He's surrounded by men, all of whom have gray hair and blue suits. They're aiming for naturally sharp, like a Dressmann fashion ad (not as handsome though).

Pervert, I think while sending him a dirty look. Then I turn to Linda and the girls. I try to figure out what people they're talking about right now. Some woman who has been charged with embezzlement. Possibly their former teacher? They're wondering if she'll go to prison.

Then there's a tap on my shoulder.

I know who it is before I turn around. Of course, it's him. *The pervert.*

"You," he says.

He is standing unnecessarily close to me. I retreat a step, feeling the women behind me squeeze together, forming a line at my back. It gives me courage to cross my arms and glare at him from under brows that I have raised in contemptuous question.

But when I take a better look at him, my shoulders relax. Because he doesn't look like he's going to say something disgusting and sleazy. He's not here to pinch my ass.

"I thought you were . . ."

He goes quiet. My hands fall to my sides.

Then Linda steps in front of me, puts her hand on the man's suit-covered bicep, and squeezes gently.

"Már," she says softly. "This is her sister. Iðunn."

13

I've been through this before. I always find it uncomfortable. And now Már is just sitting there looking at me as if he's never seen a person before. His gaze slides up and down my face, settling on my chin, lips, nose, eyes, hair. He looks at my hands, my shoulders, but he's too much of a gentleman to look at my breasts.

I know he's comparing us. He's matching his memories of my sister to my face. To my body. He's wondering if she would look like this if she had lived.

I take a sip from one of the two glasses of white wine standing on the table in front of me. He insisted on buying me a drink. Then he found a seat for us in the corner.

"He's nice," Linda whispered to me before we sat down. "You don't have to be afraid of him."

It was lovely of her to say, but unnecessary. I'm not afraid of him. I mostly feel sorry for him. Especially after he started crying. It was a very masculine sort of weeping. His eyes watered, there were a few shudders across his broad shoulders; he squeezed his eyes closed, pinched his nose as if he were trying to stop a nosebleed, and then inhaled sharply. He's recovered now, although his eyes are still rimmed in red.

They are a beautiful color, mottled, almost green. And the longer they stare at me, the greener they seem to become, as if they were moss and I was water.

"So you guys knew each other?" I ask as his regard and the silence becomes embarrassing.

He smiles apologetically. Looks into my eyes. Looks at *me,* not her.

"Yes. We were a couple. Or . . . maybe that's an exaggeration. But at least we were together."

I nod.

"How much younger are you?"

"Two years. Almost."

"And she never told you about me?"

I shrug. I remember how she would wake me up when she came home from college parties, how she sat on the floor, laid her cheek on my bed, closed her eyes, and then told me everything that had happened. Where the pre-party was. Who flirted with her. Who tried to kiss her and whom she kissed. I remember the sweet smell of alcohol lingering on her breath. The smell of smoke from her hair that sometimes remained in my bed when she had disappeared into her own and I was left alone, awake in the dark to wonder if the same adventures awaited me when I got older.

"She would talk about boys. But I don't remember any names."

"I was enchanted with her." The moss-green eyes gaze sadly out into the night darkness on the other side of the large windows. I see one bright star (Venus?).

I clear my throat. I take another sip of white wine.

"But then I graduated from MR, applied to a university in Vienna and . . . shortly afterward I heard that . . ."

He looks down. He has cuff links (real, made of gold). Már reaches for his beer, takes a big sip, and when he looks up, he looks me straight in the eye. "It was very sad."

"Yes."

"Were there only you two sisters?"

"Yes."

"It must have been a great loss."

"It was . . ." I say and quickly fall silent. Because I had almost let out something I was not going to say. Something about relief. Something about the pressure that disappeared, only to come back a thousand times over. Something about emptiness.

Már looks at me with a furrowed brow. A kind consideration fairly drips from him.

"It was a big shock, yes."

Then we sit together in silence. But it's not at all unpleasant. When we say goodbye, there is a bright green gleam in his eyes.

14

I'm exhausted when I wake up. But I'm not *only* exhausted. I have aches all over my body. I feel like I've been helping someone move.

Stumbling into the kitchen, I pour a giant glass of water. I drink it in one stretch and refill it. As I turn on the faucet, I notice that I'm still wearing my watch. 16,543 steps. I stare at the numbers. I had looked at the watch in the restaurant where I met Linda and the others. By then I'd walked almost 8,000 steps. At most, it was 2,000 steps from the restaurant to the bar. At *most*. And I took a taxi home.

The skin around my wrist crawls, as if the watch were alive, a disgusting creature suckling on my flesh. Parasites, leeches. I claw at the band, trying to free myself. The watch falls to the floor. Rubbing my wrist, the skin that had been under the watch is moist and warm. My fingers are dirty. Something brown has accumulated in dark crusts under my nails and at my cuticles. I lift my fingers to my nose. There's a smell of rust on them.

I turn on the tap again, squeezing dishwashing liquid into my palm.

The water turns pinkish when the stuff under my nails gets wet. It takes a long time to clean it all off.

HALF AN HOUR later, I have a brainstorm. Maybe the watch isn't broken? Maybe I'm sleepwalking? That could explain so much. Such as why I never wake up rested. Why I have bruises. Maybe I fall asleep and then get back on my feet without knowing it and . . . what? Walk? Back and forth in my room? Thousands of steps?

I take two Panodil, order a pizza, and then start googling.

Four percent of adults sleepwalk. Sleepwalking tends to run in families. I don't know of anyone in my family who sleepwalks. But four percent. That's a lot.

> People sleepwalk with their eyes open. But it does not look like being awake. Sleepwalkers often think they are somewhere other than where they really are. Most people go back to bed voluntarily, and when they wake up, they usually do not remember the night's events.

It fits everything. This must be what's going on. I'm so relieved. Until I come across a study that says:

> Adult sleepwalking is a potentially serious condition that can involve violent behavior. 58% of study participants had been violent at least once during their sleep. Of these, 17% had been

severely injured in their sleep or harmed a relative
so badly that they needed medical attention.
Injuries included bruises, nosebleeds, and
fractures. One participant had broken several bones
and suffered severe ankle injuries after jumping
out of a third-floor window in his sleep.

It makes me break out into a cold sweat and my heart starts pounding. Good thing it's not possible to fully open the skylight on the slanted roof of my bedroom. For the first time since I moved here, I'm thankful that there is no balcony in the apartment. I scroll over the text again. Hold on: *violent behavior*. I've never been violent. Never in my life. I never even bit anyone in kindergarten. I never fought my sister.

She hit me, but I never hit back. I just started yelling and complaining to my mom.

Then I remember the bloodstain on my chin. Where did that come from? But that wasn't blood. Of course, it wasn't blood. It was just . . . a spot of sauce that I overlooked when I went to bed. And the stuff on my hands when I woke up. That was the soap from the club. I used the bathroom before I left. The soap was in a golden can. It was thick and smelled weird. I probably hadn't rinsed my hands well enough. Right? I was a little drunk and I was in a hurry.

But nausea rises in my throat. I swallow, take a few deep breaths, and remind myself that sleepwalking is undoubtedly better than getting an incurable neuro-degenerative disease.

A thousand times better. A million times better. I steel my mind and keep reading. It turns out that the risk factors for sleepwalking are: stress, intense emotions, insomnia, drug and alcohol use, and strenuous exercise. It says nothing about solutions or healing.

I continue to google, searching for solutions. There is talk of cognitive behavioral therapy and sedatives.

I want medicine. Immediately.

But it's Saturday. I can't call Ásdís's house, can I? No. I cannot. I just have to wait until Monday.

They recommend trying to get your sleep routine in order, like going to bed at the same time every night and waking up at the same time. They also recommend locking doors and windows, as well as storing weapons and knives in a safe place.

I stare at the screen, thinking about all the knives in the kitchen drawers. They definitely haven't been moved? Right?

When the doorbell rings, I jump. The pizza is here.

15

I call the health center at eight o'clock. I get a return call from Ásdís at noon. I thank God that, as a resident, she's not as busy as the "real" doctors (I do not believe in God). I had gotten to work and had kept reading about sleepwalking—in academic terms, it's usually called somnambulism, which I think sounds like some kind of cannibalism—until the phone rang at 11:47.

I jump up, lock myself inside the toilet, and answer.

"Yeeeesss," says Ásdís when I have painted the picture. "I don't know whether that—"

I intervene before she denies me sleeping pills.

"I have to try. I *have* to. I'm exhausted. I can't keep going like this. And it's got to be this. It fits everything!"

"Drugs are not the first solution to sleep problems," she says, and I can feel my stomach tightening. "It's important to get to the root of the problem. I'd like to try other ways first. Have you met the psychologist I recommended?"

"No. Although I did just read that cognitive behavioral therapy can work. But I have to get sleeping pills.

Can't I do both? I promise I'll book an appointment with him immediately."

In her hesitation, I can feel that she is of two minds.

"Please. I'm at the end of my rope." I don't have to pretend to be choked up. I mean what I say.

Ásdís sighs, "All right."

It's like my life is suddenly bathed in a golden glow. I knew I could count on her. I *knew* it.

"Really?" I ask in a low voice, just so I can hear her say it again.

"Yes. I'm posting a prescription on the medical portal for a month. Let's start with that. Why don't you book a telemedicine appointment with me and we'll see how things are going then?"

I squeeze my eyes shut to hold back the tears. "Yes." I am overflowing with gratitude.

"No problem."

I hang up and look at the tired woman in the bathroom mirror. I blow my nose and clean off the mascara that's smudged below my eyes.

"Goodbye, bags," I whisper, and smile.

The reflection does not reply.

WHEN I SIT at my desk again, I'm gripped by the notion that Ásdís might change her mind. Maybe she decides that she should consult with a more experienced doctor (for example, the male doctor who thinks that women's troubles are all in their head) and he disagrees with her diagnosis, rubbing in her inexperience and embarrassing her for prescribing this drug. And since the prescription is electronic, there would be nothing to prevent it from being revoked before I can have it filled at the pharmacy. So clearly, I have to go immediately to get my prescription.

There's an old man in front of me in the pharmacy. He is rambling and walking with a cane, and on his pants are stains that look suspiciously like piss. He stops at the counter, rummaging in his wallet for a prescription. I want to push him aside, screaming (I do not). When it's finally my turn, I give my ID number with a quavering voice.

The prescription is still in the system. I want to kiss the hands of the young man who hands me the white paper bag (I do not).

IN THE EVENING, I change the sheets and take one white tablet. While I wait for it to work, I soak in the tub, brush my hair a hundred strokes, apply the expensive cream I never use, and then climb under my smooth, clean blanket.

I feel peace and tranquility in my heart. As if everything is whole. *I'm* whole.

I take a deep breath, turn off the light, lie down on the pillow, and close my eyes.

16

I wake up. Lying still, I relish the loosening of the last silk ribbons of sleep and try to assess how I feel. A bit like the captain of a spaceship that has jumped through a wormhole; for a moment, reality has darkened, and a thousand different futures stretch around me as possibilities. For now, the ship has appeared on the other side, seemingly undamaged. The captain takes a serious look at the viewscreen covering the wall in front of her, at the unexplored stars flashing ahead, and says: *Status report.*

Then the reports come in from fingers, arms, toes, and feet.

I can hardly believe it, but . . . I have no pain anywhere. It could still be an illusion. Often, it's not until I move that I feel tired and heavy. So, I take a deep breath—the spaceship captain clenches her jaw—and lift my arm.

It's light. There's no burning in my muscles, no fatigue. I lift my other arm, and then I sit up. I'm a little dizzy and have a strange taste in my mouth, but according to the package instructions I read yesterday, those are common side effects of the drugs. Otherwise, I feel good. *I feel good.*

I get to my feet. My eyes fill with tears.

And then I start laughing.

ALL DAY I look forward to the evening. I can hardly wait to take this little white pill that has—literally overnight—revolutionized my life. I want to call Ásdís and tell her everything in an easy rambling conversation (I do not). I'm wondering if I should call someone else. Linda? Ásta? Or maybe put something in our private friends' group on Facebook where they're all constantly sharing news. But I feel like I don't want to. I want to keep this to myself a little longer. I suspect pregnant women feel like this sometimes. Keep the secret for a few days, in order to hold something warm and soft in your heart, all alone. I would seriously like to write a love letter to the pharmaceutical giant that produced the drug. Or try to find the Facebook page of the person who developed it. Tell them that they saved my life (I do not).

It briefly occurs to me that it's not normal to have no one close enough to share such a feeling with. Except for Ásdís. But the thought's uncomfortable, so I shove it away.

I don't have time to think about anything like that. Not today. I have something else to think about. Because now, I feel like I have a future. That it can hold adventures—even magic—around the corner. That maybe I can have a *beautiful life*.

"You're really happy," says Stína after lunch. There is an accusing note in her voice as she sits and stares at me suspiciously. I evaluate her in return, contemplating how awful that lipstick is for her skin tone and how she has too much foundation between her eyes. But then I decide to demonstrate generosity and kindness. Be a bigger person than usual. So, I smile and shrug.

This seems to annoy her even more.

"Did you go to that masturbation class?"

"No," I say. "What masturbation class?"

"They did a whole segment about it on Smartland."

"Uh-huh."

Her shoulders tense up. Maybe she would benefit from getting a massage. Or taking a masturbation course.

"Then why are you so happy?"

"I just slept well." I smile, and then I continue to work.

When I look up a little later, our eyes meet over our computer screens.

Stína sniffs and hunches over her keyboard.

I wonder if I'm the person she compares herself to when she feels like shit and thinks: *At least I'm not like Iðunn.*

When I turn into my street, Mávur is sitting on the fence at number 28. I say kiskis, reach out my hand, and walk toward him. Mávur is always happy to see me.

I also know where he likes to be scratched (in the back of the neck, behind the right ear).

Usually, he starts purring as soon as he notices me. But now he's staring at me. His pupils expand into dark voids as he arches his back. His tail poofs out like a wire brush. He turns sideways to look bigger. Then he carefully retreats two steps, jumps off the fence, and slinks behind the house.

My hand drops. I stare after him for a moment. What exactly is the deal with my cat friends? But even the weird behavior of Mávur (my oldest friend in the neighborhood) does not significantly affect me. Because I'm whole. The stars are still sparkling in front of me, brilliant with the promise of a beautiful life.

The only difficulty I have now is counting down the hours and then the minutes until I can take another sleeping pill. It's a holy moment when I swallow it.

It lifts me up in a light embrace. I lie down on the soft pillow, wrap the blanket around myself, and sigh happily. Then I close my eyes and fall asleep.

17

I awake on the kitchen floor. The light outside is bleak and gray. I am shivering from the cold and my right leg aches. When I drag myself to my feet, I see a large bruise on my hip, another smaller one on my thigh, and a third on my knee as though I had fallen on my side. I look around in a daze, trying to figure out what happened. The kitchen cabinet over me is open. The cabinet where I keep the sleeping pills. And am I imagining it, or are they slightly closer to the edge of the shelf than where I left them last night?

A feeling of dread hovers over me for the rest of the day. I took a pill, but I still ended up sleepwalking. And what had I intended to do? Was I headed to take another sleeping pill? Or was I trying to get into the knife drawer? It's empty. I moved all the knives.

My leg hurts all day.

I come to the realization that it's not just twinkling stars ahead of me. There's also the dark between them.

I TRY MY best to ward off thoughts of the void—the fundamental meaningless nature of life and the truth that despite the choices we make every day we all still die. I focus on the pill I'm going to take tonight. How it is perfectly shaped. Smooth and round and white as the driven snow.

My leg is still hurting when I take the pill. The dark tries to force its way into my consciousness, like some monster lying in wait beyond the translucent stretched-skin windows of a turf house. Half-buried and isolated, I feel the thin membrane that separates me from the darkness distend—but it doesn't rupture. I'm aware of the dark now, and the moment is no longer holy. I drink some water, considering for a moment. Then I take another pill from the pack and ruin its perfect shape, breaking it in two. I swallow one half. I put the other in the pack, and the pack in the box, and the box in the cabinet.

18

I wake up in my bed. Not actually on the pillow, and I'm only half under the covers. But the ship has come out of the wormhole. The captain gets up from her chair, steps forward: *Status report.*

There's no pain anywhere. Except for a little in my leg when I stand, aftermath of the previous night's fall. I'm not tired. Just a little groggy and with a bad taste in my mouth, but everything is within expected parameters. I take a deep breath. Let myself hope.

The day is good. The evening too. Until I open the kitchen cupboard and take down the medicine box.

All the pill packs are empty. The sleeping pills are gone.

19

I set up my phone on the bottom shelf of the bedroom closet, the one above the drawers, where I store sweaters. It's a bit of a hassle to place it so the camera faces the bed. I make sure there's enough space in the phone's memory, and I plug it in before I start the video recorder. I lie and dim the lamp but do not turn it off before I try to sleep.

20

My thigh muscles are sore when I get out of bed the next morning. My fingers ache when I pick up the phone. It's hot after being charged all night. I stop the recording, then sit on the bed and play it. The screen shows a picture of the bed. I'm lying on my back. I watch myself lie still for over a minute. In the image, I rolled onto my side, so my face was turned away from the camera. My shoulder blade protruded into the air. My breathing became deeper, more regular. I twitched and then I fell asleep.

I watch myself sleep for a whole minute. Then I fast-forward. I'd been sleeping for thirty-three minutes when I moved again. I stop fast-forwarding. My past self lay on my back. Then I watch myself as I sat up. I swung my legs over the bed, my soles on the floor. Facing the camera, I looked down. My face was in the shadows, but it seemed expressionless. I started rocking in my seat. My past self rocked for three minutes. Then I got to my feet and walked out of the picture.

I stare at the empty bed on the screen. Continue

fast-forwarding for ten minutes. The blank bed is like a still photo on the screen. I increase the fast-foward speed. Minutes pass. I speed it up. The minutes become an hour and then another. Three hours and forty-three minutes after I got up, I walked back into the picture. I watch myself sit on the bed. My feet rested on the floor. Then I lifted them into bed, spread the blanket over myself, and lay down on my side. My face was turned away from the camera. My shoulder blade protruded into the air. My breathing was deep and regular.

I rewind. Freeze the video at the moment when I was sitting with my feet on the floor and facing the camera.

I zoom in on my face. It was in the shadows but I can still see my eyes.

They were open. Attentive.

21

Where did I go?

22

I cannot stop looking at the screenshot I took. At my face just before I went back to bed. It does not look like the face of a sleeping person. The gaze is not dreamy. It's vigilant. Focused.

As if someone is in power. Someone other than me.

And that's not the worst.

The worst thing about this expression is that I know it. It may have been a long time—but I've seen it before.

23

I set the phone back up in my closet the next night, the night after, and then the third night. I record three more videos. They're all the same. Except the last.

When I came back and sat on the bed, I looked up and straight into the phone.

And I—*if this is me*—smiled. Then I got to my feet, stretched out my arm, and closed the closet. Everything went black.

I rewind. Freeze the image on the smile.

That unbearable, contemptuous smile I thought I would never see again.

24

I'm standing in the checkout line at Krónan, waiting to pay for my groceries, when my phone rings. I don't recognize the number, so I let it go to voicemail. The phone continues to ring in my coat pocket, and I feel the vibration as I'm handing my stuff to the checkout clerk, but it's stopped by the time I bag my groceries.

I'm crossing the street at Ánanaust when the phone vibrates again. I check it. There's a message from the same number.

> Hello. This is Már. I wanted to thank you for talking with me the other night and to ask if maybe you'd be willing to meet again?

25

"I hope I didn't come across as desperate, asking to meet on the same day that I called?" Már laughs but there's a vulnerability in his green eyes that makes me think he isn't completely joking.

"Not at all," I say, and he seems relieved. "It's been ages since I've gone out to eat."

"Same here, and just . . . thank you for saying yes."

"No problem."

There is still a problem. I had to think about saying yes. For the last few days, a constant hurricane has been raging in my head. I've had a hard time thinking about anything except what's really been happening to me at night. At the same time, I can hardly bear to think about it either (avoidance?). My head is constantly filled with a steady bubbling that drowns all other thoughts as fast as they rise out of the morass.

I need to find a fixed point in the storm. And for some reason it occurred to me that Már could become that point (why?). In a worst case scenario, this evening could be a welcome distraction.

"It was amazing to meet you that evening," he says. "But then I came home and realized that I had monopolized the conversation. Talking about me, and about your sister. And I realized we hadn't really discussed you."

Sometimes I imagine that if I say little enough, people will find me mysterious. That they'll begin to imagine that I have this rich inner life. That I think deeply but have no need to show off, that my ideas are too precious for careless babble, that I carefully select where I choose to shine.

I want to be like . . . There was this silent man at a party I once went to somewhere near Vesturbæjarlaugin. He barely said a word all night but still everything revolved around him. The women tried to catch his eye, the men tried to make him laugh. But he just sat there silently—and for some reason we were all convinced that he must be the smartest man in the room.

I have gradually come to the conclusion that this tactic only works for men. If you are a woman who is silent, then people assume you're stupid and have nothing remarkable to say.

And in my case, that's true.

I'm scared shitless when I meet people who relentlessly pluck at the veil I sometimes imagine myself wrapped in, teasing it aside with each intrusive question on the heels of another, until there is nothing left but my naked self, which does not want to be pitied any more than Loki in chains.

"There's not much to discuss," I say cautiously.

I tell him what high school I went to, what I learned in college. Where I work. Where I live. Where I went on my last summer vacation. Then I turn the conversation back to him.

And to my relief, he takes the bait without hesitation.

I sit back in my seat and take my time studying him. He's wearing a blue jacket, white shirt, and cuff links. But it's not the same outfit as last time. His hair is starting to turn gray, but he's still young. His skin is smooth and matches the warm cream of the wall behind him. He looks like he lives in this nice, expensive restaurant.

When we finish our meal, we get dessert and coffee.

When he invites me to his house, I say yes.

26

Már lives on the east side of the harbor in the chic high-rises that have sprung up around the Harpa Concert Hall. The apartment is brand new and tastefully decorated. I even think I can smell paint, but that seems unlikely, since he says he's lived there for nine months. He opens a bottle of champagne, and as he pours it, I walk to the huge north window. I admire the marina, the small open motorboats rocking gently by the floating docks. Over the sea, the moon is in the clouds, and the mountain Esja is like a sleeping giant—I know she's there but I can't see her in the dark.

When Már embraces me from behind and starts kissing me on the neck, in front of that enormous window, it's as if we were standing on a stage, and when I turn around, I feel like I'm performing. My mouth finds him and I start to unbutton his shirt.

Már smells good.

Már has soft lips.

Már has a thick beard, which scratches my chin.

Már has a broad chest.

Már has a slightly crooked penis; it points up and slightly to the right (five minutes past twelve).

Már goes down on me on the couch and I come twice.

Már leads me into a room.

Már wants to do it with the lights on. His bedroom window is the same size as the living room window, and I can't get rid of the feeling that we're onstage, that we're not alone at all, so I say no.

Már understands that.

Már turns off the lights.

I know I can't fall asleep. But it's so tempting. The bedding is thick and soft, like in an expensive hotel. We lie close together, my buttocks against his groin, my back against his chest. He has one arm under my head and the other lies over my waist. When I feel reality slowly fading away, I open my eyes. I sit up. Már startles.

"I can't fall asleep," I say.

"Why not?" He sounds disappointed. Like I hurt him.

"Because . . ." I swallow. "Because I have to wake up early in the morning. I have to show up early. At work. And I want to take a shower and change my clothes."

"Are you sure? It's so nice here, cuddling like this."

"I'm sure," I say without looking into his eyes.

Már does not try to make me change my mind (what a prince!).

The moon has broken out of the clouds. I watch it as I get dressed, the way the moonlight glistens on the black crests of the waves and how it falls on Esja, the long shadows it drapes over ravines and crevices.

I feel Már's gaze on my back as I wriggle into my dress.

I glance over my shoulder and see him pulling on his shirt.

"Don't get up."

"I'll just see you to the door."

"No. You were asleep. I can let myself out."

I walk to the bed, lean down, and kiss him on the temple. The skin there is warmer and softer than I expected. He closes his eyes. When he opens them, he looks at me and smiles sadly. "Can we do this again?"

THE FRONT DOOR closes quietly behind me. The streets are empty. The whole city is asleep. I go home and meet no one. Not a person, not a car. The only sign of life is when I turn onto my street and see a cat disappearing under a fence.

27

I can't go to work. As I stare into the mirror, my fingers go weak. My toothbrush slips out of them and falls into the sink.

I have a huge black eye. It wasn't there when I went to bed. There's a cut under my eyebrow, and the area around my eye is hot and tender to the touch.

I walk away from the mirror. Standing in front of the heavy dresser I dragged across the front door before going to bed, I bend down. Carefully, I consider the gap between it and the door. It's wider than it was last night. I pushed the dresser as close to the door as I could before going to bed, flush against the frame. I crouch on my haunches. There are at least two centimeters between the dresser and the frame. Someone had moved it last night.

Her.

How DID I get a black eye?

I can't go to work like this. Maybe I can cover it with

makeup? I try. Apply moisturizer, then makeup, then powder. It hurts. It's throbbing when I'm done, but all things considered, I'm pleased with the result. It looks a little swollen but the discoloration isn't obvious, especially after I apply makeup to my other eye. Maybe it's not visible if you don't know about it?

The morning sky is gray and cloudy, but I still wear sunglasses when I leave the house. At work, no one seems to notice.

I can't shake the feeling that I was punished for putting the dresser in front of the door.

28

Where did I go?

29

I'm late for dinner with Mom and Dad. I'd completely forgotten the invitation, until my mother texted me at five o'clock and asked if I was eating chicken these days?

I can imagine her in the grocery store, standing in front of the refrigerator section. She's reaching for a packet of chicken breasts when a little thing scratches her memory. She hesitates. She decides to pull out her phone, texts me, and then puts the chicken in the basket anyway, without waiting for a response. Because when I answer: No, I've told you this.

I get back: Oh, lovebug, I'm finished at the store and already in the car.

At work, I go into the kitchen and rummage through half-empty packages of crispbread and water biscuits until I find an old packet of oatmeal with apples and cinnamon deep inside the cupboard. I turn on the electric kettle, pour the oats into a cup, and eat it without milk.

Before I leave, I powder my eye again.

———

Mom serves chicken fajitas. Fortunately, there are plenty of side dishes. Again, my parents and I are following the careful steps of a family evening, which rarely veers from its set path. We're talking about my job (no news there), Dad's back (bad), Mom's thinking about trying golf (will never happen). When I pick up the plate with the last slice of avocado and ask if they care if I finish it (so polite), my mother eyes me.

"You're so tired, lovebug. A little puffy around the eyes. Are you not sleeping well enough?"

Since I woke up, I've been wishing that I hadn't had LASIK so I could wear glasses.

Mom knows I don't sleep well. And she knows I don't like talking about it, and I know she doesn't like to either. I shrug it off.

"What were you doing yesterday?"

And before I know it, my outing with Már has us swung off the dance floor of our choreographed conversation and I've lost the rhythm. "I went out to eat."

My mother brightens with interest. She looks at Dad, who isn't paying attention to anything except the chicken on the plate in front of him. Mom twitches. I know she's kicking him under the table. She does it often and thinks no one knows about her tricks. Dad flinches, looks up, and glances at her with a question in his eyes.

Mom nods at me.

"Iðunn went out to eat yesterday," she says out of the corner of her mouth, directing the words at Dad. Then to me: "With whom?"

"His name is Már."

"Már?"

"Thorfinnsson."

"Where is he from?"

"I don't know. I met him at a bar with Linda. He went to college with her and Ingunn. Two years older than them."

"Oh, really?"

"Yes."

"And what does this man do?"

I try to remember what he told me. Does he work with investments? Or in a bank? Or in an investment bank? Was he building something? Or investing in some construction project?

"Buildings . . . something."

Now Dad's interested.

"Is he an engineer?"

"Something like that."

"And did he know her, our Ingunn?" Mother asks with a dreamy expression.

I nod. It doesn't occur to me to tell my parents that they had been dating. I know what Ingunn would say if she knew. Or, rather, I know she wouldn't say anything. She would laugh. And then she would make a face.

"How fun," Mom says, smiling.

"You would have made a good engineer," Dad tells me. "You were always building something when you were little. And all those houses you drew! I don't understand why you went to business school."

"What nonsense," Mom says. "She always wanted to study business."

I chew the avocado I just picked up, shaking my head. I'm about to say that I actually wanted to be an architect, but when I swallow and look at my mother, the words die on my lips. Mom's eyes rest on me but they have a distant look and I know she's not looking at me but at *her*.

Ingunn always wanted to be a CEO.

Before she died, all roads were open to me. After she died there was only one.

30

When I get home, I download the watch app to my phone. Then I turn on the GPS location feature and put the watch on my wrist before going to bed.

31

I went to the Grandi harbor district on the west shore.
Then I went back home.

32

I buy a padlock and a latch. The woman who helps me is constantly staring at me through glasses, which have slipped down to crouch on the tip of her nose. I hadn't bothered to put makeup on my black eye—which has now turned green and yellow—and I know what she's thinking. But she says nothing.

When I get home, I screw the latch onto the door and the door frame. After I brush my teeth, I lock myself inside with the padlock. Then I lock the key to the padlock in a drawer and put the key to the drawer on top of the fan above the stove.

I'm in bed but haven't turned off the light yet when my phone beeps. I startle. I haven't heard from Már since the night I didn't spend with him (is he a player? he somehow doesn't seem the type)—which is good, because then I don't have to make up an excuse to avoid him while my black eye subsides, and bad because . . . well, then maybe he is a player.

But the message isn't from Már. It's from—*hell*. It's from Stefán. I had deleted him from Messenger so that his messages would go to the "others" box because then I can read them without him knowing. This one reads:

> My dear. I've been thinking about writing to you for a long time but I didn't know what to say. Then I realized that, of course, there is only one thing I can say: I'm sorry. Forgive me, please. And also I want to add this: Would you possibly consider meeting me again? I think we need to talk about what happened. Please. I'm sorry for everything.

I read the message twice and my stomach tightens into a hard knot. How dare he? *How dare he?*

The last time we talked, I told him I no longer wanted to sleep with a married man, and he hissed that I was a bitch just before he slammed the door in my face.

I'm considering writing something disgusting back. Something nasty. That he is embarrassingly poor in bed and that I have HIV and herpes and hepatitis and that I came across his wife swimming and told her everything in front of his children and that I've called the police and told them that he pushed me down the stairs. But I decide to wait until I've come up with something truly repulsive. Less is more and all that. It's been my experience so far that it's always better to sleep a little on such poisoned darts, before you let them fly.

Instead, I send Már a text. Decide to keep it simple.
Thanks for the evening.

I'm considering adding: I've been thinking of you, but I don't.

He answers immediately. He must have been sitting with the phone in his hand (on the toilet?).

> Likewise! I'm glad you contacted me, I didn't want to be pushy, so I've been trying to give you space. :)

I'm looking at the phone. What happened to men taking the initiative? But of course, they are cautious these days, poor things, trying not to seem too aggressive. Or at least some of them. Hell, Stefán would have benefited from maybe getting some tips from Már (he is a prince!). I think about the night at his house. The two orgasms on the couch. How many of them were in bed? Three? I notice that it is five minutes past twelve, and I feel a tingling in my abdomen. I write: Should we get together again soon?

The answer comes immediately: Absolutely! When?

Then I remember the black eye.

Soon. I'm kinda busy these days. I'll be in touch.

Good night, beautiful.

I turn off the lights. Lie on the pillow. Prepare myself for . . . I don't know what.

And that's the worst. The uncertainty. The fear that there might be nothing wrong—that it might all be just in my head.

33

I wake up with blood oozing from my fingers. There's blood on my quilt, on my pillow, on my shirt. My arms are weak, my palms ache, and my nails are torn to pieces. I stagger down the hall. There's blood on the door, where I've clawed at the lock and latch. It's been torn off the frame. On the floor is a crooked metal hasp, covered in blood.

I sit on the sofa, with a piece of cloth and a bowl of warm water in my lap. One nail (middle finger, right hand) has completely disappeared. At least three others are loose. The pain comes in waves. I soak my fingers, staring down at the water, which gradually turns pink like rose water. But it does not smell sweet—it smells of iron and salt.

34

I had taken another route, but I'd gone back out to walk along the Grandi harbor.

35

I call in sick to work. I can't type on a keyboard with bandages on all my fingers.

All my energy goes into trying to control my fears. But the dark between the stars, that empty nowhere, the void——it presses against my shields. I feel the universe expand. When the shields are about to collapse, I put on my coat and run out with untied shoes.

I've gone a long way before I realize where I'm going. To Ármúli. To the Psychology Institute where Þórir Skúlason (the psychologist who looks like a handball player) works.

I DO NOT have an appointment. The woman at the front desk inspects me, skeptical. I'm wearing a nightgown under my coat. Under the nightgown, I'm wearing sweatpants from an old boyfriend (Tommi, who just disappeared one day). I wrap the coat tightly around me. The woman looks at my fingers, at the bandages. I see the battle that takes place inside her. Suspicion and compassion are at war. Compassion wins. The woman sighs.

"I'll see what I can do." She turns to the computer, clicks something with the mouse, wrinkles her forehead, and pouts. I notice that she's forgotten to blot her lipstick (common mistake). Then she turns to me.

"There was actually a cancellation this morning. I'll check if Hákon is willing to fit you in. But it's not for another fifty minutes, if you can wait."

"Hákon? Isn't Þórir available?"

Her gaze hardens. I feel like I've crossed a line.

"No, that's great," I say quickly, shaking my head. Trying to smile. "Hákon. Yes please. That would be wonderful. Thanks."

She tells me to take a seat in the waiting room. I sit down. The man opposite looks at my hands. I put them in my pockets. Pretend I don't see him. I look out the window. There is a beautiful view of Esja. The shadows that covered the slopes when I was at Már's house have disappeared. I wonder if I will get to see them from that perspective again.

Fifty minutes later my name is called.

HÁKON IS SMALL and narrow, with a long neck and a large larynx that bobs up and down as he speaks. He looks ridiculously young, and there is something about him that reminds me of rodents. I don't find him particularly reassuring. Don't good psychologists need experience? But then I remember my encounters with prejudiced old doctors. And about the junior doctors who work so hard. Maybe Hákon is like that. I need someone with an open mind.

It's surprisingly cozy in his office. All the furniture is from IKEA (is it sad that I know that?). He even has a candle lit that smells of vanilla, yet is somehow not too aggressive (miracle), and he invites me to sit in a chair that has a blanket folded over one arm. Am I supposed to spread it over my knees? Or my shoulders? I sit and do neither.

"Well, Iðunn." He smiles. "How are you?"

I cross my arms on my lap. I see him notice the bandages. And then I tell him everything.

He listens silently. Writes something in a small book. To my great surprise, I have no interest in seeing what.

When I'm done, he wrinkles his forehead. "And you think you're sleepwalking?"

I shake my head and whisper, "No."

"What do you think, then?"

And this is the first time I dare to say the thought.

The first time I dare say it out loud: "I don't think it's me. I think it's someone else."

But I'm afraid to tell him who.

36

Hákon wants me to go to the psychiatric ward. He talks about psychosis. I want him to give me sleeping pills. Strong sleeping pills. He says he can't prescribe anything (I should have known) but that I can get sleeping pills in the psychiatric ward. The thought is tempting. To let go, just put it all in someone else's hands. Allowing doctors to take responsibility for this. For me. For *her*.

The thought of being locked inside is also tempting. I want someone to give me sleeping pills and then lock me in. Behind a framed steel door, behind bulletproof glass. Because I do not want to go out to Grandi. That district is an industrial blight. I do not want to know what's out there at the harbor.

But I'm scared. Afraid of what will happen if I don't go there. If *she* doesn't go there. What she'll do to try. How she'll take revenge next time.

Because this is my body. What happens to it if it's thrown at a steel door? Repeatedly?

"If I go, do you think I can ask for a straitjacket?"

Sadness sweeps across Hákon's face and he doesn't

answer my question. He just repeats that he feels I should go there. Immediately. He offers to call a taxi for me.

I refuse the taxi but promise Hákon that I'll think about it.

I think about it as I walk west. Then I go home.

37

I don't lock the door when I go to bed. And don't lock it the next night nor the next after that. I wake up exhausted each morning. But my fingers are starting to heal.

I sleep with my watch on, but after four nights I stop looking at the map when I wake up.

I don't always follow the same path. But I always go out to the harbor at Grandi.

38

What is out at Grandi?

39

Goddamn Stefán keeps sending me messages. The man does *not* know how to take a hint. I haven't had the energy to think of anything disgusting enough to answer him with. And perhaps the most provoking option would be to ignore him altogether. Isn't indifference worse than hatred? I feel like I've read that somewhere, but my head is fuzzy and stuffed with cotton. It's hard to think clearly.

To be clear, I'm aware that my head is not *literally* full of cotton. It's full of fat and blood. It's as if all of that has solidified into a ball of hard glue.

Hákon (who does not look like a handball player) calls me. I tell him I've decided not to go to the psychiatric ward. I tell him I'm sleeping well. I tell him I'm doing well. I hear the doubt when he asks if I'm telling the truth, if I'm completely, completely sure. The suspicion that I'm lying to him colors his voice. I hear this, even though I don't know him at all (maybe *I* should have become a psychologist).

And to be honest, I don't put a ton of effort into trying to convince him. I know that he knows it doesn't matter what he believes or does not believe. It's not like he can deprive me of my autonomy or call my mom (right?). I repeat everything again.

I also hear the hope in his voice that he's wrong. The hope that I'm telling the truth. I hear the hope getting stronger. Like he's trying to reassure both of us that I'm okay.

Truly, it's a little reassuring to hear him repeating, "You are okay?" over and over again until it almost stops sounding like a question and more like a statement.

When we say goodbye, I almost feel like it's maybe true. But that doesn't last very long.

I'VE BEEN HOME for over a week when the human resources manager calls me. It's a quarter past eleven, but I'm still lying in bed, gross and with dirty hair. The HR manager says that I'm well on my way to using up my sick days.

"Are you . . . ?" she says gently, and then lets the question fade into soft silence.

I know what she's doing. She wants to ask what's wrong with me—and I know she thinks a mental illness of some sort—but I'm pretty sure she can't ask what it is, and I'm sure she knows it and that she's hoping I'll fill in the silence and tell her everything in an unsolicited rush. Because people can't tolerate silence. Not even a soft silence on the phone. Silences are, of course, worse in person, and most people will do anything to fill them, especially women. Centuries of socialization have conditioned us into believing that it's our responsibility to create a cozy atmosphere and ensure that no one is embarrassed about anything. That's why we laugh at jokes that offend us. That's why we smile at people who pat us on the butt. That's why we pretend that it's just a coincidence when the boss repeatedly brushes against our breasts at work. Because anything else would be just so embarrassing. *For everybody.*

I have been trained to smooth out all the imperfections, the same way other women have. But I'm too tired to be bothered by the silence on the phone. I don't have the energy to be embarrassed. I just lie there and listen to the silence get longer as I stare into the air and think about how tired I am. Fatigue even fills the hand holding the phone to my ear, and the gravity well drags it down as if it weighs at least five kilos.

When her interrogation technique fails, the human resources manager changes tactics and says that I should submit a doctor's note if I don't start to get better. I thank her, say I'm feeling better now, at least I'm better than I was the day before, and hopefully I can come tomorrow—or the day after. When she hangs up, I let the phone drop to the pillow.

I lie there a little longer, looking up at the ceiling. Then I get up (taut cords of pain in my thighs, back tight) and take a shower. While shampooing my hair, I decide to shake off my malaise. I mean, just because someone (or something) takes control of me while I sleep doesn't mean I can no longer live life, does it?

I call Már and invite him to visit.

40

My apartment smells like a cleaning commercial. I swept, mopped the floors, scrubbed the kitchen with Ajax, the bathroom with a paste that I never know what to call, then I changed the sheets, and put the shirt and underwear I've been wearing for the last week through the hot cycle in the washer.

I'm tired afterward, which is nothing new, but what surprises me is that I'm no more tired than usual. As I paint my eyes and put on lipstick, I wonder if the girls might have been right after all? Maybe I just need to exert myself and meet people and then I'll feel better. So, while I remember that the problem is no longer just unexplained fatigue—it's something else and more— I've decided not to think about it tonight. Tonight, I'm going to live life. I'm going to live quite a lot. I apply mascara. My black eye is gone. I'm missing two nails (another fell off two days after the padlock) but there's nothing I can do about it now.

At eight o'clock, the bell rings. I push the buzzer on the intercom, go to the stairwell, and bend over the railing so I can look down at Már's head as he climbs the stairs. His hair is not thinning (he is a prince! But not like the British type).

He smiles as he takes the turn on the landing below and notices me. I toss my hair over my other shoulder and smile back. We kiss before he takes off his jacket (a little tongue), and the corner of the paper bag he's carrying sticks under my skirt, scratching my bare thigh. I invite him in, learning that the bag contains burgers, fries, and a bottle of red wine, which I suspect is very expensive.

Már is a gentleman (and a prince!) and walks around the apartment, praising the view and looking at the pictures on the walls but—I am not a lady and I want to do it right away, not after we've been dropped into a food coma by burgers and french fries and red wine. He doesn't protest when I go straight to work and make my intentions clear.

THE BURGERS ARE cold and the fries are soggy when we finally eat, but the red wine is very good. I drink my first glass fast and it warms my stomach. It hits me hard. We only talk about the weather, last week's news (I need to keep an eye on it), and then Már suggests that we watch a movie, something South American on Netflix that his friend recommended.

I hand him the multitude of remote controls that it takes to work the television, and he navigates them with no problem (how?). But he can't find the film, can't remember the title, and has to send a message to a friend and then call when he doesn't answer the message. I relax on the couch and wait patiently while his friend spells the title for him. When the film starts, Már sits beside me and drapes his arm along the sofa behind me. I sigh and rest my head on his shoulder.

This is nice, I think. To live such a life.

41

I wake up in my bed. I'm not alone. I stare up at the ceiling, then turn my head. Már is asleep next to me. My heart starts pounding in my chest so fast that the beating becomes a boil that roils in a cold sweat over my body. I must have fallen asleep on the couch. I must have fallen asleep and I don't remember anything.

I sit up. And then a thought flashes through my head. Már is dead and I have killed him. No. *She* has done it.

I hold my breath. Már lies on his side with his back to me. He has beautiful shoulders. Shaped and tanned.

His shoulder rises slightly with his breath.

I collapse beside him.

I'm so relieved that he's only sleeping that I dissolve into a boneless heap. I let out my breath, empty my lungs completely, and then wish I could stop filling them again.

I don't want to do this anymore.

But then Már stirs. He rolls onto his back, turns his head to me. His eyes are still closed. I breathe in, a shuddering breath that may or may not be the beginning of crying, and he opens his eyes. They are green and more beautiful than I remembered and it seems to take them a moment to focus on me.

Már smiles. Then he rolls to face me, raises his hand and brushes my hair away from my face.

"Good morning," he murmurs. "Come here."

He slips his hand under my neck and pulls me close to him. I close my eyes, digging my nose into his chest. He smells good.

"Good morning, my dear." He nuzzles the hair at the nape of my neck. "And thank you for last night. The second time . . . Iðunn." He laughs. "You are absolutely amazing."

He embraces me tightly and I clench my fists.

42

I wake up with seaweed in my hair and black sand between my toes.

43

I do not want to know what's out there at Grandi.

44

I wake up with blood on my right knee. The blood is clotted and brown and it is not mine.

45

I need to know what's out on Grandi.

46

I transfer the GPS coordinates from my watch to the computer. It takes awhile but in the end I manage to overlay all the night trips on one map.

I always walk the same way out to Örfirisey: down Holtsgata and then north along Ánanaust. There the red lines branch off. Sometimes I walk Fiskislóð, sometimes Grandagarður, sometimes I follow the harbor bank to the east and sometimes I go down to the shore. I study the red lines. It's as if someone has taken a pen and scribbled over the middle of Örfirisey. I clear all the night trips away. Start again with the blank map. I layer them on top of each other. Each wrinkled ring road trodding on the other's feet. And then I see it.

The point where all the lines overlap.

47

The HR manager calls me. My sick days are coming to an end. She says that I can apply for unpaid leave and also apply for disability benefits. She tells me to talk to my union, I have rights there. I thank her for the tip and tell her that I actually think I'm improving.

"You said that when I last spoke to you," she says accusingly (am I imagining the tone?).

"Yes, but then I had a setback. Now I'm working through that and I'm getting much better."

She's starts in again. "Have you been under the care of a doctor?"

"What?" I say, just to delay a little. Because I'm uncomfortable that—

"Have you sought any help, Iðunn?"

It's inevitable. "Yes." I have to lie. "Of course, I did."

Then I realize she's led me into a trap.

"Good to hear. It should be easy for you to get a doctor's note to submit to us." I can hear the sugary smile in her voice.

"Well, yes, of course," I stammer.

"Great. Good talking to you. Take care of yourself."

I hang up.

Now I've got even less desire to go back to work. Basically, zero. It's hard to imagine anything I'd like to do less. And the HR manager won't give up until I submit this "doctor's note." I feel it in my bones. There's only one thing to do. I'll have to quit my job. I have to resign. No—I should apply for the disability benefit she mentioned. Go on leave. Yes. I'll do that.

I browse the website. View the application form. A doctor's letter must be submitted.

I swallow. I don't dare to call Ásdís. I can't. Not my Ásdís. Maybe I could have called right after the sleeping pills disappeared. Or maybe when I woke up with a black eye. Even after I talked to Hákon. But it's too late to do it now. Because I broke faith with her. We had a confidential relationship. She was on my side. But now I've betrayed her trust and it's too late.

48

Of course, goddamn Stefán is the first person I meet
when I return to work. He's standing in the lobby waiting for the elevator. He must have heard the automatic
door open for me because he turns around and looks
at me. I stop. There's no one else in the lobby so he has
no excuse for not talking to me—after the first time we
kissed he stopped greeting me at work (smooth). I'm
thinking about turning around and going home, but it
was hard enough to force myself to get dressed and get
out of the house, and if I go home now, I won't come
back tomorrow, let alone the next day or the one after
that or after that. And Stefán does not own this place.
He may sound like a domestic rooster, but this is not his
domain. I've worked here longer than he has.

I lower my chin and walk into the lobby.

"Iðunn," he says.

I do not look up.

"Iðunn," he says.

I walk on, turning toward the stairs.

"Iðunn." He steps in front of me.

I twist past him but Stefán rams his arm out and clamps on to mine. Hard.

I look up. "Let me go."

He raises an eyebrow in question.

"You're hurting me."

He looks down at his hand, as if surprised to see it around my upper arm. He releases his grip. And then he makes this concerned face, like it's awful to discover that he "accidentally" hurt me. As if I should now feel sorry for him. I want to lash out at him (I do not). Instead, I walk again.

"Iðunn," he calls after me. "Iðunn, why didn't you reply to my message?"

I'm on the stairs. I don't look over my shoulder. I walk upstairs and almost feel like I hear him say, "I miss you," but maybe it's just my footsteps echoing in the stairwell.

49

I'm standing by a high fence. I look at my watch, where I entered the coordinates for the Dot. Where all lines overlap. It's inside this. But where? I see rusty containers, flimsy sheds, wire rolls, barrels, grease. This is an industrial area but no industry seems to have happened here for a long time. The fence isn't that high. It should be easy to climb over it. I look around. I'm north of Krónan and Nettó, so there's no shopping traffic here. But still, there are way too many pedestrians. A young man walks with a pram. An elderly couple with a dog. Jogger. Two men cycling in overly tight pants. And a few cars.

I'll have to come back tonight. In the dark.

50

When it gets dark, I take off my dress and switch into jeans and a wool sweater. I pull on hiking boots and a coat and stuff my leather mittens in my pocket. Then I walk down to Grandi.

There is no one on the street. Not even the weirdos who come here in the shelter of night to drive fast. Still, I look around carefully before pulling on my mittens to protect my hands and climb over the fence.

Nobody notices me. I take off one mitten and look at my watch. The Dot is somewhere ahead. I walk carefully. In front of me are two rusty containers. Between them stands a flimsy shed. I examine the shed carefully and something about it nags deep in my consciousness. I cautiously move closer.

The wood is faded and there are remnants of paint in an indistinguishable color. The entrance to the shed is sloping and a sagging door hangs from its upper hinge and juts into the doorway. Inside there is deep darkness.

I realize two things:

1. I should have brought a flashlight.

2. The darkness in there is the darkness between the stars. The darkness that has tried to penetrate my consciousness, and presses on my defenses. If I go in, I will tear apart the membrane that has separated us. The Dot on the map is not just coordinates. This is a turning point.

If I walk into the dark there will be no turning back.

But I don't have to go into the dark. There is a flashlight on my phone. I put my hand in my pocket, pull out my phone, and turn on the light. The beam is faint, but when it falls on the shed I see that the peeling paint is green and that inside the doorframe, deep in the blackness, something is glistening.

I do breathing exercises that I learned on YouTube, trying to control my lungs, which are sucking in the air with such desperation that I start feeling dizzy. I force myself to take a slow, deep breath. And as my heartbeat slows, I face the truth: it's too late.

Whatever has hooked me has a helluva grip on me. The hook is already so deep in my flesh, that the only way out is through.

I walk into the darkness.

51

There is a brooch on the floor. A silvery curve with en-crusted gemstones glinting in the beam from the phone. Around the pin are spirals of stones. The light flashes on something else. It falls on a lighter. Polished shards of glass. An earring. A silver condom wrapper. And more spirals of stones.

Inside the shed is a large puddle. The water is red with mud. I catch a glimmer of something off-white in the murk, but as soon as I spot it, I am certain that I don't want to know what's lying there.

I take a picture of the pin and the pebbles. And also the other stuff.

I light up the wall in front of me. Kelp has been strung up on the rotten wood. The smell of iron, salt, and wet soil fills my mind. It is invasive. Something is disintegrating, rotting. I think I can detect a pattern in the purple kelp. Another spiral. Many spirals in differ-ent sizes.

I take a picture.

Something catches the dim light. Something is

hanging up to my right. I light up the corner. There's something furry. There's a glimmer of green light and for a moment I think the creature is moving. But then I see that its eyes are cloudy and broken. What were indistinct lines merge into a familiar form.

A cat hangs on a leash that has been tied around one leg. Its yellow-striped coat is blood clotted. I trace the lines on the wall and realize why the puddle is red.

Then I see the collar around the cat's neck. It is blue with pink hearts, and I would recognize it anywhere. *Mávur.*

I back away, drive my elbow into the crooked doorframe, and drop my phone. It lands facedown and the beam of light shines through the abyss above me. My eyes are drawn to the light; I look up, stare open-mouthed at all the broken, gleaming eyes. A drop falls on my lower lip. I taste iron and salt. I gasp, snatch my phone, and run out.

52

Why didn't I notice how many cats were missing? I scroll across the neighborhood page on Facebook. Virtually every other post is about a lost cat. Many of my friends are there: Sushi, Brendingur, Hjálmar, Lúsí, Tígra, Sólveig Hrund, Núðla, Þengill, Snotra, Malar, Eyvindur, Ófétið hann Jón, Nala, Lúlú, Mía, Sól, Mjáa, Brundur, Kattgeir, Snati, Rækja, Loppa, Elvis, Branda, Saffó, Bríet, Svarthöfði, Skratti. And Mávur. In the photo posted by his owner (a famous drummer), he is lying on a sofa. A small hand, which must belong to a child, strokes Mávur's head. His green eyes droop with pleasure, and though it's not visible in the picture, it's clear that he is purring. The collar he wears around his neck seems to be brand new, the polyester hasn't started to wear out. It is bluer than I remembered and the pink hearts are brighter. The color goes especially well with his tawny coat.

Bile rises in my throat. I clamp a hand over my mouth, jumping to my feet, but I can't get into the kitchen in time and vomit on my living room floor.

53

She killed those cats.

54

I'm afraid to look at the pictures I took.

55

I'm afraid to go to bed.

56

I must have fallen asleep on the couch sometime in the morning. I wake up in bed.

My watch is gone.

My phone is gone.

57

Someone has to tell all those people where their cats are. Because nothing is worse than uncertainty. I know that myself.

58

Except in some cases. In some cases, the certainty may be worse.

59

I killed those cats.

60

But what if there is nothing out there at Grandi? Maybe I hallucinated this? If I had the nerve to look at the pictures, would they have shown an empty shed? A blank wall? But now my phone is gone and it's too late to know.

I open the computer, reading the posts about the lost cats over and over again. The thought of a shed full of cat carcasses is becoming more and more absurd. I haven't dreamed for many months but surely I must have dreamed this.

Right?

These people need to know if something has happened to their cats. *I* need to know if something happened to their cats.

It takes me two days to steel myself enough to return to Grandi. I have decided that if I find anything, I'll create a new account on Facebook, under a pseudonym, and send the police a message that I have seen a dead cat on the plot. Can the police track it down?

Maybe it's safer to just post something on the neighborhood page?

I STAND BY the fence, looking around. It's approaching midnight. I smell smoke somewhere north of me and hear the squeal of the tires echoing between the houses, but I don't see anyone. When I'm sure no one is watching me, I climb over the fence. I pick up my flashlight and walk to the shed.

It's empty. But the puddle is still there. The water is red.

61

I buy a new phone. When I turn it on, my inbox is filled with text messages. How many days have passed since the other disappeared?

Four? Five?

Mom's been trying to invite me to dinner. She asks if I eat turkey; there's a deal on frozen breasts at Melabúðin. Ásta highly recommends a series on Netflix. Már wants to meet me. And, goddamn Stefán is still at it.

I remember, once, I decided I was going to live life.

It was nice while it lasted.

I answer Már.

He invites me out to dinner.

62

I feel like Már is surprised when he sees me. But he's a gentleman (and a prince!) and says nothing. I tell him I'm exhausted and have been sick. He shows sympathy, asks gentle questions, and mentions that I've lost a little weight.

"Thanks," I say (a conditioned response).

He makes a strange expression, for a moment, as if that had not been a compliment. I am reminded that the reason I am wearing a sports bra under my dress is that all my regular bras have become too big for me. The patriarchy whispers to me that no man wants to sleep with a woman who is too skinny. *Who wants to get a pointy hip bone in the groin when he's trying to fuck you? Nobody wants to do that with a skeleton.*

The patriarchy speaks with my mother's voice.

Már asks what I want to drink.

"Beer, " I say (fattening).

I feel like I have to prove I don't have an eating disorder, so I order halibut in cream sauce, rinse it down with another big beer, and when he suggests we share a dessert, I say I want my own.

Már opens a bottle of red wine when we get to his house. As he pours for us, I stare out the window. It's cloudy. No Esja, no moon, no stars. Just darkness.

I'm too full to have sex, so I tell him I want to chat a little. We sit on the couch, and he invites me to put my feet on his lap.

Then he starts rubbing my feet and talking about my sister.

"It must have been a terrible shock," he says. "When Ingunn died."

"Yes." I think of my mother's stiff face as she told me the news and the silence that swallowed my dad like quicksand and how I stopped being able to sleep except for in her bed.

"It was a shock to me," he says. "And I can't even say that I knew her well. Not the way you did. I can't imagine how it must have been for your family. For you. And to die like that . . ." He is silent. "I've actually read that it's the most peaceful form of death. In such cold water, you'd probably just feel pleasantly tired. Some people don't even want to be saved. Fight back. And you . . . you don't know if she meant to . . . or if it was just . . . ?"

He looks at me. I'm in a hurry to shake my head. Trying not to think about what I found under her pillow. What I haven't told anyone about.

He looks down, nodding. "Of course, it's a crime that there aren't fences by the harbor."

Már presses his thumb under the ball of my foot,

moves it in ever-expanding circles, then lifts his finger and starts again in the middle of the sole. *Pressure, relief, emptiness*. I start thinking about the spirals in the shed, the smallest one I saw. Now I feel like he was in the middle of the wall, right in front of me. A dark spiral, surrounded by other dark spirals. The darkness in its center was pitch-black. As if there were not just a shadow but a deep hole that led to . . .

"It was just such a loss."

I look at Már. His green eyes stare vacantly into the living room. I know he's picturing her. I want to know what he imagines. What she looks like in his eyes. Is she walking down the hall at school, with earrings in her ears, a bag hanging on one shoulder, and books in her arms? Is she at a dance? In a long dress, blond hair straightened, rings on each finger and a pendant hanging from her neck? She always liked sparkly things. Or is she lying naked in his bed?

I do not have many pictures of her in my mind. I remember the wrinkle between her eyes when she screamed at me after I damaged her flat iron when I was thirteen and she fifteen. I remember her long fingers, which were always so cold. And I remember the scornful tone she kept especially for me.

"She was so beautiful, so smart, so funny, so charming," says Már. "She was so talented and she had her whole life ahead of her. It was so unfair. That she was snatched from us. Sometimes I think about what she would have been doing now, if she had lived." Már's thumb rests on my heel. "Do you think about that too?"

The unfathomable form I perceived in the dark takes shape. An icy cold certainty pours over me. I do not have to wonder what she would be doing now.

I know.

Már stares at me. At *me*. His green eyes remind me of Mávur. The pupils expand and the moment stretches.

"Iðunn?" There is a worried wrinkle on his forehead and his voice is gentle. "I'm sorry. Of course, you feel uncomfortable talking about her. You don't need to."

I move closer to him. I lean toward him and kiss him on the mouth.

63

I wake up in my bed.

64

I'm afraid to call him.

65

I'm going to send him a message.

But I don't know what happened.

What should I say?

What tone should I use?

66

Dear Már. I don't quite remember how last night ended. I think I drank a little too much. If I crossed any lines, I apologize for that.

67

He does not answer.

68

He does not answer.

69

He does not answer.

70

Surely she has not . . .

71

Surely *I* have not . . .

72

I call him. He hangs up without speaking. At first, I'm relieved. Because at least he's alive. But then the relief gives way to something else.

A darkness carves through my chest in a downward spiral.

73

I call back. Again. And again.

And then again and again and again.

I put my phone on the table.

I turn on the TV but I keep an eye on my phone constantly.

I'm watching it when the screen lights up and beeps.

My heart is pounding when I see that the message is from Már.

> Stop calling me. Stop sending me messages.
> Leave me alone, or I'll call the police.

74

Two more kittens have disappeared. Krínólína and Api.

Krínólína is a fine little girl, white with black spots. One spot covers her ear and half her head and resembles an alpine hat at an angle. Her nose is tiny and pale pink in color.

Api has gray markings. He is tall-legged and slender like a Siamese.

When it gets dark, I go back to Grandi.

The shed is empty.

75

I buy another smart watch. This time I fasten it to my
ankle. I tape the whole strap with electrical tape before
going to bed.

76

I wake up in my bed. My ankle is bloody and full of cuts.

The watch is gone.

My wounds sting when I take a shower.

The water in the shower base turns pink like rose water.

When I rub shampoo into my hair, I feel a massive knot in the back of my head.

11

I've decided to stop sleeping.

78

I pour myself coffee when I get home from work. At eleven o'clock I go grocery shopping at Nettó and fill my basket with energy drinks. When I get home, I open all the windows, then place my most uncomfortable chair in front of the TV to watch a series about divorced people. The actor who plays the husband is gorgeous. I want to lick his chest. I pause the episode, pick up my vibrator, and masturbate with a picture of him frozen on-screen.

At four o'clock, I finish the series. I go for a long walk.

When it's done, I take laundry out of the washing machine.

I'm even pretty cheerful when I get to work. Despite the fact that Stefán's come up to our floor to help my boss with something on the computer. I can plainly see him glaring at me, but I just pretend not to see him. I pretend he does not exist.

On the way home, I buy Indian food, ask for their

spiciest dish. As I stand outside my door at home, I realize that I have not spotted a single cat on the way.

I POUR MYSELF coffee at ten o'clock and put in another load of laundry. I clean the bathroom, scrub the floors, and then take all the pictures off the walls and wipe the frames. At four o'clock I go for a walk. I arrive at work at half past six.

79

I don't think I need to sleep.

80

I haven't felt this good for *months*. Maybe I should just sell my bed?

81

Setback. The third night is devilish. When I almost fall asleep washing the dishes, I go for a walk. I put in my earbuds to listen to an audiobook, a bloody thriller, and walk all night. I arrive at work at eight o'clock. Stína does not even try to hide her feelings when she sees me.

"Iðunn! You look awful!" she chirps. "Did something happen?"

"No."

The disappointment darkens her eyes like a cloud across the sun.

She was hoping for some gossip. That my mom was dead or that I had run someone over, or maybe I had gotten my heart broken and would break down here in front of the coffee machine (caffeine) and tell her everything. I almost feel sorry for disappointing her.

At lunch I go to the swimming pool and use the cold tub. While drying my hair, I consider whether I should try to obtain some drugs (speed? cocaine? Molly? heroin?). I don't even know what they're called, let alone where I can get them. I understand there are some

Facebook pages and even apps (I saw that in a news story), but I don't have any idea where I should start looking and it's not like I can ask someone.

When it's five o'clock I decide to work late.

Because if I go home now, I'll fall asleep. When I'm finally alone in the office (Stína raised an eyebrow before she left, as if to indicate that she sees all the way through my act) I get an energy drink, then I sit in front of the computer, open YouTube, and watch videos of shark attacks.

I'm not going to spend the night here. I'm just going to stay a little late.

Because when you stop sleeping, there are suddenly so terribly many hours of the day.

82

I wake up to a sound. I sit up, wipe the saliva on the corner of my mouth, and look around confused. My computer is asleep and it's dark inside the office. Do the lights go out automatically at a certain time? I've never been here later than six. I move the computer mouse to wake the screen up and I see to my great relief that it is only five minutes past eight. I've slept no more than twenty minutes.

Then I hear it again, the sound that woke me up. A low click and thump.

I get up.

The light inside the printer room is on. At first, I think the sound is coming from one of the printers but then I see someone in there. Someone is standing by the copier. When I realize who it is, I stop in my tracks, and I'm going to back out of the hallway as quietly as I can, but it's too late. He's heard me. Stefán turns around, and from his expression, he's surprised. We stare into each other's eyes.

The surprise on his face gives way to a smile. It seems completely sincere, but it still fills me with loathing.

"Iðunn! Are you here? God, you surprised me, I thought I was alone in the building. The photocopier downstairs is broken."

Then he just stands and stares at me. When he raises both eyebrows in question, making three deep wrinkles form on his forehead, I realize that he expects me to say something. I decide not to indulge him.

He waits a moment longer and then says, "Are you angling for a promotion?" Judging by his tone, he finds that unlikely.

"Yes. Goodbye."

I'm turning to escape. I have only taken five steps when I hear Stefán coming after me.

"Iðunn," he says. "Iðunn, wait."

I expect to be grabbed by the shoulder and am so surprised when it doesn't happen that I turn around.

Stefán has stopped. He's a few steps away from me.

"Please," he begs. "Can we talk?"

I inspect him slowly. Then I sigh.

I don't want to deal with him at all. But it's still better than falling asleep.

83

We go to a pool hall that I had no idea existed. It is on the east side of the city, crammed between a furniture shop and a garage. Stefán says that he comes there sometimes, but I don't believe it. He doesn't fit in here, dressed in a suit and with gelled hair amid all the beardy hipsters. But I know why he chose this place; no one knows us. Because Stefán is married and I know that he doesn't have the slightest desire to leave his wife, regardless of anything he's said to me. I also don't want him to leave her. Not for me.

I never asked him to, but he still talked about it as if it were the plan. Starting with the third time we slept together. It's as though he were in a play and thought this was the way to commit adultery. And I didn't bother to correct him, as I'm not an expert in adultery even though I've been involved in affairs before.

I knew full well that Stefán didn't care about me. And I felt the same.

Sometimes I wonder why I had bothered with the relationship. Because it's not like I thought he was irresistible. I thought he was fairly handsome (before I got to know him), at least compared to the other louts who work with us. But Stefán is not charming, he is not funny, he is not entertaining, he is not smart, and he is not good in bed. He was not kind to me. He's never sincere, he's just parroting something he's seen actors say in movies, and he never really means anything he says. Which made me realize something sad. I had just been bored. Stefán showed an interest in me, and I had nothing better to do.

That's why I was startled by how he reacted when I broke things off. At the fury which ignited like I'd flicked a switch. He couldn't handle me rejecting him. He would have beaten me if we had been alone. I'm sure of that.

Now he's sitting opposite me, on a worn-out bench, looking at me as if I were some wonder that had slipped out of his grasp. I realize he's rewritten our history. Rewritten me. I've always thought it was a myth that the best way to turn men on is to reject them. But clearly not as far as Stefán is concerned.

I cross my arms. "What do you want to talk about?"

He pulls himself together. "May I get you something?"

"Coke," I say (caffeine).

"Nothing with . . . alcohol?" he asks, and I know he's trying to soften me up.

"You can pour a little rum into it."

I watch him walk to the bar. His shoulders are

stooped like he's carrying the devil there, as if he were a much older man. He orders. The bartender, who is tall, narrow, with a long beard, and even longer hair under a red cowl, puts a large beer and a glass of Coke on the table. No garnishes. Not even a lemon. Stefán pays and then holds his wallet for a long time, seeming to struggle with something.

I look away as he turns around. Pick up my phone and pretend to be looking at something there. Because I know he will interpret my gaze as being admiring. As if I can't help but long for him.

He puts the glass of Coke down in front of me. I look up.

Stefán takes a big sip of the beer and then he sighs.

His upper lip is sweaty. He's nervous.

For a moment I feel sorry for him, but only one. "Well. What did you want to talk about?"

"How's your drink?"

I take a sip. At first, I only get the sweet taste of the coke, then I taste bitterness at the back of my tongue. I swallow and grin as the heat from the rum warms my throat. "There's a weird taste to it."

"Yeah, the bartender actually mentioned it. This is a new rum they're testing. He said it wasn't for everyone. Can I try?"

He picks up my glass without waiting for an answer, takes a sip.

But he just barely wets his lips and doesn't even need to swallow.

"It's not bad." He hands the glass back to me.

I take another sip. The bitter taste is still there, but you can get used to anything. And I need caffeine and I need sugar.

When I look up, Stefán looks at me with something like excitement. And I'm a little sad that our relationship hadn't included his current longing for me.

"Are we going to talk about something or not?"

"Cheers first," he says. "It's really nice to see you."

I roll my eyes but raise a toast with him. When we lower our glasses, he suddenly becomes serious. It's obviously that time.

"I just wanted to tell you that I'm sad about how things ended between us. And I also wanted to tell you that I miss you."

I start laughing and shaking my head, but it suddenly feels so heavy that I can't straighten it again. It just starts to droop to the other side. I feel my eyes rolling in their sockets and my face turns to dough.

"I . . . I feel . . ." But my tongue has become too big for my mouth, like a piece of meat between my teeth.

I try to shake my head again, but I bite my tongue. I taste blood but feel no pain.

Stefán watches me with interest for a moment.

"Come on." He gets to his feet, leans over me, and grabs my other arm. He pulls me to my feet.

"Whaaa tha helllll?" I try to stand, but my legs won't support me. I try to ask to go to the hospital but what comes out is. "Sspiralll."

He tightens his grip so I don't slip to the floor. "There we go . . ." he says, a little breathless.

My head sags to the side, resting on his shoulder. The last thing I see are my legs, the right one dragging along the floor like it's paralyzed while Stefán carries me out.

84

I wake up in my bed.

My hands are covered in blood.

85

I'm afraid to call Stefán.

86

"You look much better than yesterday," says Stína when I come to work. "Did you sleep well?"

I mumble something into my chest while slouching away. Then I go to the bathroom and wash my hands. The skin is red and dry. I've scrubbed my hands several times with a brush and dishwashing liquid, between all my fingers and under my nails. Then I cut my nails and scrubbed my hands again with vinegar (deodorant), but the metallic smell still clings to them.

I disinfect my hands, then sit at my computer and try to calm down.

Just before noon, Stína comes to me, obviously bursting with gossip. She bends close and whispers: "Stefán has disappeared!"

87

I sleep. I wake. The day passes.

88

I sleep. I wake. The day passes.

89

My phone rings. A woman introduces herself as Þóra Hjálmtýsdóttir, a police detective. She asks me to come to the station after work.

90

The room does not look like one of the interrogation rooms you see in movies. There is no steel table screwed to the floor. There is no mirror wall, no ashtray, but there is a camera in one corner.

It looks like any other office. It's a bit shabby, and the upholstery on the chair that Þóra invites me to sit on is torn, exposing the dirty foam inside, but otherwise it's just an ordinary office chair.

The table is just a desk with a computer and a dusty potted flower. There's even a painting on the wall (ugly).

My palms are sweating and my mouth is dry.

Þóra Hjálmtýsdóttir is older than I expected. She has blond, bleached hair, black eyebrows, and is very muscular. She must have a motorcycle, a big dog, and a boyfriend twenty years her junior.

"All right," she says. "As you know, we're investigating a missing persons report. Stefán Þór Hallvarðsson has not been seen since Thursday."

I did not know he had a middle name. I almost tell her that, but then I decide it does not matter.

"You knew each other," she says.

"Yes."

"You were in a relationship."

"Yes. But that ended before . . ." How long ago? I can't possibly remember.

Þóra watches me patiently. I try to smile and shake my head.

I tell her the truth. "I'm sorry, I don't exactly remember how long it's been over. I haven't been sleeping well lately. It's hard to think clearly when you're sleep deprived."

She nods.

"You ended it? The relationship?"

"Yes."

"And he was opposed to that?"

"Yes."

"We've received information from his mobile carrier and we've also looked on his social media. He repeatedly tried to contact you over the last few weeks."

"Yes. But I didn't answer him. It was completely over for me."

She nods. Then leans forward. "But you still saw him? You worked together, right?"

"Of course, I saw him at work. But I tried to avoid him. We never talked."

"And you don't know where he is?"

She looks at me, her gaze watchful, as if she isn't just waiting for an answer but measuring my responses at the same time. Like she's a human lie detector (is that possible?).

I tell her the truth.

"I don't know where he is."

Þóra nods. Then she smiles and stands up. I'm relieved. The interview is clearly over. "Thank you for coming."

"No problem," I stammer. Then I can't help myself and ask, "You . . . you don't know where he is?"

"No." Then she rolls her eyes, lowers her voice, and says in a conspiratorial tone, "Truth to tell, I don't think anything's happened. People sometimes disappear. And he, he was not . . ."

She lets the words fade out. Allows the silence to fill in the blanks.

"I see," I say. "Okay. Got it."

Þóra accompanies me to the front door of the police station. We say goodbye and I walk out into the darkness.

91

I sleep in the dark. I wake in the dark. The day passes in the dark.

92

The phone rings.

Linda asks, "Have you seen the news?"

93

Már is missing.

94

I stand by the high fence. Inside it, I can make out the shape of the shed, the Dot, where all the lines overlap. *Overlapped.* I climb over the fence. Then I go to the shed. It's empty. The puddle has even disappeared—evaporated.

I go out again. Look around me. One of the shipping containers is open, its door half ajar. Inside the doorway is darkness.

And I know. Immediately.

I turn on the flashlight and walk inside.

95

The first thing I notice is the brooch on the floor. The pebbles lie around it in a tight spiral.

I shine my light in the right corner.

Stefán hangs on his clasped hands. They are tied together with blue string. The skin around the cord is purple. His eyes are closed, and his face is white.

There's a wound on his neck, slashed at a diagonal, like a horrifying grin. His white shirt is covered in blood.

I catch my breath and take a step back. My heel lands on something slippery. I stumble, trying to regain my balance, but I'm standing on something wet and slick. My feet slip out from under me. I fall backward.

My head hits the floor.

96

The pungent smell of iron and salt fills the shed. There's something wet under my cheek, something cold.

I have a splitting headache.

I open my eyes.

The first thing I see is a shaft of light. The flashlight is next to me, right in front of one hand. If I stretched out my fingers, I could touch it. The light falls on the bed of kelp that I'm lying on. I follow the light with my eyes, all the way to a pair of men's black shoes.

I sit up. The headache escalates, drilling into my head like an ice needle. I squeeze my eyes shut, letting the pain flow over me in waves. When the worst is over, I open my eyes again and reach for the flashlight.

I shine it on the shoe. There is a foot in it. I move the light up the leg, to the knees, thighs, brown belt, black jacket, neck, and face.

Már is gagged. His eyes gleam in the darkness like two green pearls.

"Már," I say, and at the same time, I see his eyes widen with fear.

Fear of her. Fear of *me*.

His hands are tied. All I have to do is look at the knot to realize that I can't release him with my bare hands. I need something sharp.

Maybe there's something in here, something I can use.

I turn around too fast. Pain drops on my head like I've been struck by lightning. The pain grips my neck and crawls down my spinal cord in a fiery path. The world tips to the side, and I lose consciousness—but only for a moment.

When I come back to myself, I hear a sound.

Someone is muttering in the dark behind me.

The voice is familiar, and I feel the hair on the back of my neck rise.

I clench the flashlight and then turn around carefully.

97

She is sitting on her haunches in the corner next to the door. Her face is hidden behind the long fingers of her hands. Blond and long, her hair is dirty and drapes around her shoulders.

I stop in front of her. The murmur is monotonous as if she were reciting something or saying a prayer. I can't distinguish the words.

I stare down at her blond hair, at her bony, curved back. The peaks of her vertebrae protrude from her pale skin like the tops of a mountain range. I can see ribs under her off-white skin. Her breathing is regular and deep, as if she is asleep.

I fall to my knees in front of her.

With that, my neck spasms. Pain bites my head. My eyes tighten again and I scream.

98

I open my eyes. The murmuring has stopped. I look up.

She has raised her head and lowered her palms. Now she sits and looks at me. Her cheekbones are higher than I remembered, her lips thicker, her eyes bigger and pitch-black.

I hold out my hand.

Her arm is off-white and far too narrow.

She places the knife in my outstretched hand. The blade is long, and for a moment, the knife teeters in my palm until I grab the handle.

We look into each other's eyes. I know what she wants me to do.

I turn to Már. When he sees the knife in my hand, his face tightens in horror.

"Easy now," I say. "It's going to be okay."

The knife is sharp. The blade cuts so gently.

99

She's waiting for me outside the container. I stop in front of her. Walk one step closer. My shoulder touches her shoulder. We are exactly the same height.

I take another step, stretch out my arms, and hug her to me. She's so cold. Our bones touch, our hips collide, I dig my nose into her pale skin and take a deep breath. My senses are filled with the smell of iron, salt, and cold.

I've thought so many times about what I would say to her. But I say nothing.

Instead, I lift her on my back. When I walk away, her feet hit my calves. She doesn't really weigh anything.

I stop at the fence. I can't climb over.

She extends her white arm and points. Then I see it. There's a hole in the fence. I head there.

As I sneak through, I hear a sound behind me.

I don't look back. I know it's Már. I had cut the ties, and now I have to trust that he'll get out on his own.

I cross the empty street. There is no one about. The streetlights cast golden pools on the asphalt.

She puts her cold arms around my neck.

100

I can smell the ocean before I hear it. The wind is cool from the north and blows our hair back. The beach is rocky. My foot slips once, twice, three times. She tightens her grip on my neck, and I do not fall.

I step down into the soft, black sand.

I think of the footprints we leave behind.

Above the tideline, kelp has washed ashore. The seaweed is slippery underfoot, but I don't lose my balance.

The sea surges midway up my calf.

She puts her cheek to my cheek. It is cold, as cold as the sea that now reaches my hips.

Her weight diminishes as the sea slips under her. I tighten my grip on her knees, so she doesn't slip away from me.

Then I kick off from the bottom.

I let myself float on my back. Her hands are still around my neck, her feet around my hips. I'm in her arms.

In the sky above us, the stars twinkle. Between them is the dark.

ACKNOWLEDGMENTS

First, I would like to thank my very good friend and fellow writer Alexander Vilhjálmsson for talking over this story with me at length and helping me find the shape of it before I wrote it down. Thank you also to my early readers and friends, Fjóla Kristín Guðmundsdóttir, Guðrún Lára Pétursdóttir, and Kristín Svava Tómasdóttir. My Icelandic editor, Sigþrúður Gunnarsdóttir, also worked her magic before the story's initial publication in Icelandic.

Thank you to my agent, Seth Fishman, for not being daunted by the thought of taking on an unknown writer writing in a tiny, foreign language. And thank you for sending this book to Lindsey Hall, editor at Tor Nightfire. Thank you, Lindsey, for taking a chance on Iðunn's story after reading only a few chapters, and thank you for loving it once you read the whole thing.

And last, I want to thank one of the most generous people I know, Mary Robinette Kowal. If I had not met her at IceCon (which is probably the tiniest science fiction and fantasy convention in the world) one rainy weekend in Reykjavík in the middle of a pandemic, this book would not have landed in your hands, dear reader. Not only did she ever so graciously offer to introduce me to her agent, Seth, but she also offered to translate samples of my work to send to him. Then, despite being very busy with other projects, she ended up translating this story in full. Her wonderful translation speaks for itself; it was a joy to work with her and Lindsey on it, and I truly could not be happier with it.

I don't think I will ever be able to repay Mary Robinette for her generosity, so instead I will do my best to pay it forward.

Hildur

ABOUT THE AUTHOR

HILDUR KNÚTSDÓTTIR was born in Reykjavík, Iceland, in 1984. She has lived in Spain, Germany, and Taiwan, and studied literature and creative writing at the University of Iceland. She writes fiction for both adults and teenagers, as well as short fiction, plays, and screenplays. Knútsdóttir is known for her evocative fantastical fiction and spine-chilling horror. She lives in Reykjavík with her husband, their two daughters, and a puppy called Uggi.

ABOUT THE TRANSLATOR

MARY ROBINETTE KOWAL is the author of *The Spare Man, Ghost Talkers,* the Glamourist Histories series, and the Lady Astronaut Universe. She is part of the award-winning podcast *Writing Excuses* and a four-time Hugo Award winner. Her short fiction appears in *Uncanny, Reactor,* and *Asimov's Science Fiction.* She lived in Iceland while performing for *Lazy Town* (CBS) as a professional puppeteer. *The Night Guest* is her first work of translation.